Disco Bar

Tori Ross

Author's Note

Just popping in here to say this book takes place in 1978. For those playing along, that's pushing almost fifty years ago. Please keep that in mind when reading it. Polyamorous relationships look very different now. Back then, throuples and the like were unheard of or the stuff of hippie urban legends. Even gay, lesbian, and bisexual people did not have the same rights or visibility they do today. I tried to keep true to the time.

Phones were attached to the wall.

Women ironed their hair to straighten it.

Bell-bottom pants ruled.

Quaaludes were a drug of choice.

Most importantly for this book, men could not marry men, and many things weren't publicly flaunted. Same-sex partners may not have been seen as equal to a spouse or female partner to make a medical decision or be on a financial account. Surrogacy didn't exist, and adoption was not allowed for same-sex partners. DNA tests weren't a thing.

Nicole comes from a small town and is twenty-three in this book. That means she was born in 1955, so please keep that in mind when I mention her background. Many women were told their place in society at that time, so I've tried to stay true to the narrative of a small, Midwestern town and what a devout family would have told a girl growing up at the time. Hell, I was born in 1976 and was told a lot of the same things by my grandmother. Like Nicole, I'm originally from downstate Illinois. Women of that time and age were certainly virgins, even if I normally avoid female virgins in my writing. For younger folks reading this, this book takes place only four years after the Equal Credit Act was enacted, allowing women to finally have bank accounts and credit cards without a man cosigning for them. It was a time of awakening for women. Again, I tried to keep true to the time, so I hope you don't view Nicole as weak. In fact, I think she's kind of badass for listening to her own counsel on what is comfortable for her.

You'll see.

Content Warnings: The obvious one is threesome sex. There's a double vaginal penetration scene, as well as several other positions, and Felix licks Nicole "clean" more than once. There is also an M/M scene between Felix and Dex that includes rimming. Looking at it now, Felix has no problem licking anything and everything. This book is absolutely meant for and marketed to those 18 or over! There are mentions of side character drug use and past drug use by the main male characters. I'll also add a warning about the things Nicole was told about her place in society. That can be triggering for some people with cultural trauma who have experienced the same.

Contents

Dedication IX

1. Upside Down 1

2. Turn the Beat 13

3. Wild 28

4. Help Wanted 46

5. Green with Envy 58

6. Fondue Favors 64

7. Dancing Queen 75

8. Hard Truths 82

9. Come to Felix 93

10. Date Night 102

11. Piercing Nicole 109

12. Seconds 127

13. Dance with Me 134

14. Kneed Me 144

15. Dropped 154

16. True Love 162

17. Dance Battle 169

18. Tima Talk 176

19. The Contest 183

20. Lay All Your Love on Us 196

21. Home at Last 207

22. September 1980 221

Also by 227

Acknowledgements 229

About Tori Ross 231

For the women of the 1970s who broke the cultural norms.
Thanks for the credit card.

Upside Down

Nicole

"What the hell are you doing home?" Tima asks, a milk carton halfway to her lips in front of the open fridge. She looks out our small kitchen window that's littered with half-dead herbs from my last attempt at apartment gardening, furrows her brow, and looks left to right. "It's not snowing. Did school get canceled?"

I drop my keys on the counter and sink into a nearby kitchen chair. The orange vinyl squeaks as I lean back. As soon as a tear trickles down my cheek, Tima's circling our Formica kitchen island and rubbing my back while I sniffle and rub my nose on the back of my sleeve. Polyester isn't absorbent for snot, and I look around for a tissue, only finding paper towels that are like sandpaper on my face. They'll have to do. Tima and I don't think about buying tissue for the apartment. That seems ridiculous now since we're two single roommates who have had our fair share of heartbreak, but we're twenty-three and in our first apartment. We're lucky we have dish soap and food.

"F-fired," I stammer, shaking my head like I'm trying to wake up from a bad dream.

Tima pulls back like I slapped her. "Fired? How did you get fired?" She smiles and wipes a tear off my chin. "Did you fuck the janitor in the storage closet?"

I can't help but sputter a laugh. It feels good to feel something except for failure and fear. Failure that I couldn't keep my teaching job at a religious school for more than a few months. Fear that I have no idea what I'm going to do next.

Teaching jobs are hard to come by in Chicago this year. It's like every single woman with a degree in something came out of college in the last ten years and immediately decided to get a teaching job. The position at the small school associated with a large church was all I could get. It wasn't much in pay, but it paid my half of the rent on the apartment I share with Tima, paid for my city bus pass, and my half of utilities.

"I'm not having sex with Mick," I snort, thinking about the elderly custodian. "They said I wasn't going to church enough."

"Excuse me?"

"It's a religious school. They said the teachers have to attend church every week."

"You go to church," Tima says.

I lift my head. "They're also picky about where. They don't care that I go to the Baptist church a block down every couple of weeks. They said parents want to see me in *their* pews with my hands raised every week. So not only do I have to go to church on their timetable, but I have to go to theirs."

"That's the most ridiculous and authoritarian thing I've heard of. Did you fight it?"

I sigh and straighten my shoulders. "No," I practically whisper. "I just...don't have any fight left in me."

Tima tilts her head. "What do you mean you didn't fight? You just accepted it and shrugged?"

I sniff again. "What was I going to do? There were already parents complaining about other things. I'm too lenient. I'm too strict. I give too much homework. I don't give enough homework. I had parents calling me because I gave their kid the D they earned, and their poor darling couldn't play basketball until they brought the grade up. Calling me at home, Tima. Being a teacher is like being Joan of Arc on a salary of eight thousand dollars a year."

I reach for a nearby glass and eye the jar of sun tea Tima makes on the window ledge every day, regardless of season. I pour the glass three-quarters full and think about adding a splash of rum and honey like Tima prefers.

I'm not usually a drinker, choosing to only have a sip or two of wine if I'm out at dinner, but I want something to take the edge off. I yearn for something to make me think about anything besides looking for another job. I also don't want to wrap my brain around seeing people and having to explain to them why I got fired.

The phone rings, a shrill sound cutting through the silence in the kitchen, and I startle. Tima walks to the phone, greets whoever called, and twirls the cord around her finger as she slips into the next room.

It must be nice to have friends.

I wouldn't know. Not only am I jobless, but I'm friendless. I'm new in town and don't know a soul except for Tima and the friends of hers that I've met as they traipse through the house on Saturday nights, drinking cheap bottles of wine before going out on the town. I left my friends back home when I moved three hundred miles away, and long-distance phone calls are expensive. Chicago isn't an easy city for a mouse like me to make friends in, and I catch a glimpse of myself in the wall oven glass. Fingering my hair, I study my tear-stained face and squint.

Long, brown hair, stick-straight from the iron. Pale cheeks that stay that way in the summer no matter how much baby oil I slather on my skin. Winter air certainly doesn't help except to give them a smidge of pink that only lasts for two minutes when I come inside. Mousy clothes.

I study my boring brown bell-bottom pants, my pink peasant top, and the green and brown plaid coat I'm still wearing, belted at the waist, and I immediately compare the simple outfit to Tima's wardrobe of miniskirts, boots that go up to her knees, and plenty of necklaces and bracelets. She even wears miniskirts in the winter, choosing to shiver as she waits in lines for club entry with her friends.

I finger my bare earlobes. Mom wouldn't allow me to pierce my ears or wear loud jewelry. She said it would show wealth, making me prone to mugging, or signal to a prospective husband that I'm greedy.

I need a change. Desperately.

Tima walks back into the kitchen, hangs up the phone, and smiles at me. "You're coming out with us tonight."

I stiffen. Tima's a great roommate, and we've become close in the last eight months since I moved to Chicago, but we've never gone out except to get a quick dinner. Tima has her friends. I have my embroidered pillows. We're not exactly bookends.

But to be invited to hang out with Tima and her friends...

"I don't know if that's a good idea," I say, drawing the words out.

Tima puts a hand on her hip and leans against the wall. Without speaking, she opens the kitchen drawer she uses for junk and pulls out a pack of cigarettes and a lighter. I watch as she lights a cigarette, takes a long draw off it, and blows the smoke out of her lungs into the kitchen air. I wave the smoke away, and she smirks. "Nicole, you have to get out of the house."

"I just want to feel sad for a bit."

That's not entirely true. I want to break free. I itch to do something different. Anything. Something dangerous. I eye Tima's cigarettes and wonder if I should take up the habit. I just don't know how to be someone other than who I've always been. I don't even know how to articulate my desires to the world around me. It's not in my genetic makeup. I've been told the world was one way, and I needed to adapt to it.

"Do you want to keep doing what you're doing? Being who everyone else wants you to be?" Tima asks.

No, I most certainly do not. My tongue won't work to say that, though. I've been conditioned my entire life to be who everyone else wants me to be. I feel like a snake that's desperately trying to shed its skin but can't. I often wake up from nightmares where I'm being suffocated or strangled. My entire body is telling me it wants out of...something. I have no idea what I need, but it's not whatever my life currently is.

Tima bends down like she does when her new designer jeans are too tight and she needs them to give a little. "You're coming out with us. You're borrowing an outfit from me, and you're going to get the stick out of your ass before it sets down roots and becomes a tree. You're twenty-three, but you act like you're seventy. You're coming to the club with Miriam and me tonight. No questions." She strokes a strand of hair out of my face. "You're going to dance. You're going to talk to a man." I open my mouth to protest, and she puts her index finger over my lip, startling me. "You're going to try a cigarette. I'm going to buy you a beer – maybe even some vodka shots. Have you had a white Russian?"

I raise my head and squint. "You want me to date a communist?"

Tima sputters the smoke she just inhaled and pounds on her chest with her closed fist. "No, sweetheart, a white Russian is a drink. It's not a man from the Soviet Union."

She tucks her cigarette to the side of her mouth and pulls me up with both hands. "We're going to get you dressed," she says. "Then, we'll roll and feather your hair. There's a Farrah under there somewhere." She stops and looks at me again like she's seeing me for the first time. "I mean, you have brown hair, but total Farrah."

I look down at my clothes. "I can't go like this?"

She raises an eyebrow and looks me up and down the way the girls did in the junior high bathroom. "Not if you want to actually be let *into* the club."

I let her take my hand and follow her to the bathroom. She pops a piece of gum into her mouth to get rid of the cigarette breath with one hand and turns on the bathtub with her other hand. "In you go. I'm going to find you something from my closet. Wash the hair. Shave the legs."

"It's not my normal hair-washing day," I protest. "I'll have to re-iron it."

Tima pinches her nose, shakes her head, and mumbles "Jesus fucking Christ" as she marches out of the bathroom to her room, ostensibly to find something for me to wear.

I dip my toe into the filling tub and let myself sink into the warmth. Reluctantly, I wet my hair and flip open the lid on the Agree bottle. Lathering my hair, I push away thoughts of my job. Maybe this is the right thing to do. I can't stay a quiet choir girl for the rest of my life. Tima is right. She's young and fun, manages to hold a job as a secretary, and gets a lot of male attention. I'm obviously doing something wrong.

I've never had male attention. I've kissed a few boys during some forbidden bottle-spinning games in high school, but I was always pushed away from boys who weren't husband material, even if I was fifteen. If they weren't an eventual husband as soon as I left high school, I wasn't allowed to date them. I even went to prom with my cousin because he didn't have a date. You can imagine the incest jokes.

Some things need to change. Desperately. Maybe getting fired was the kick in the ass I needed.

I rinse the shampoo from my hair, drain the tub, and put in leave-in conditioner, letting it set as I use my electric razor on my pits and legs. I glance at my bush in the mirror, wondering if I should shave it like Tima does, but she's an anomaly. Everyone I see in locker rooms and at public pools has a full bush, just trimmed at the sides so it doesn't hang out a swimming suit. It's winter. I'm fine like I am, and I can't imagine the razor burn.

When I'm combing out my hair with my towel wrapped around me, Tima knocks on the bathroom doorframe and walks in with dental floss.

At least, that's what it looks like.

"What is that?" I ask, eyeing what passes for fabric in her hands.

"It's your halter top tonight."

"Like hell." I eye the offered top and look down at my medium-sized breasts. "I don't think I'll fit one of them in that."

She shrugs and chomps. Her hair is already beautifully feathered, and I can smell the Breck hairspray in her hair. She obviously used her hot rollers while I was in the bathtub. She holds out my pants for the evening in another hand, and I momentarily forget about the top.

The pants, if they can be considered that, are dark purple and have a hint of glitter to them. I'm sure they look fantastic in the light of the club, but I don't even have underwear that'll fit me while I wear them. All I have is underwear my grandmother bought me at Sears, and I was raised to never have panty lines. A slip isn't an option here, and I search my mind to think about where I put the girdle my mother bought me before I moved to Chicago.

Should I wear a girdle? It seems like something a nice girl would do, and it keeps everything in ship shape. But I've never seen another girdle in our apartment. Tima must not wear them.

My roommate understands the dilemma, and she huffs so hard that her bangs blow out of her face. "You don't wear panties with them, Nicole."

"You want me to leave the house without panties?" I ask, my mouth hanging open after the words roll off my tongue.

"I have so much to teach you. Turn around," she says, roughly turning me by the shoulders until I'm facing the mirror.

Tima's red hair is so different from my wet locks, and her made-up face stands in stark contrast to mine which barely gets Bonnie Bell lip gloss.

Without warning, she rips the towel away from my body, and I shriek, covering myself by placing a hand over my bush and an arm across my breasts. "What is wrong with you?"

"I'm getting you ready. You need desperate help." Tima glares at me from the mirror. "You do want help, don't you?"

My naked shoulders slouch, and my eyes droop to the small makeup bag on the counter. It's all I have for cosmetics, and it only contains some simple gloss, two jars of nail polish, and a light pink blush I can't be sure even matches my skin tone.

"Yes, I want help."

A chill runs through my body in the cold bathroom air, and I'm not going to get relief from the top that Tima shoves down my raised arms, if it can even be called a top. I close my eyes, not wanting to see my own breasts or even Tima's face when *she* sees my breasts. I can't stand the judgment, and I can't remember the last time someone other than my doctor saw my body.

Wait. *Only* my doctor has seen my body.

Tima knocks on my shoulder, and I open one eye, dreading how I look. My eyes focus on the reflection in the mirror as Tima moves down my legs, taps my left calf, and helps me into the purple pants as I lift my feet.

The top is a white halter, but the sequins look pinkish in the light. I can imagine what the bar lights will do to it.

But my boobs don't look half bad. In fact, they look pretty great. I haven't yet started to sag, and the halter stops about halfway down my breasts, making a nice natural cleavage. When my pants are on, Tima taps my hands and wakes me from my thoughts so I can button and zip my own pants.

I may not be able to eat anything or sit down all night, but I don't look half bad.

Tima smirks as she watches me turn in the mirror. "Yes, you're passable. But we need to do something about your hair and makeup."

I gesture to my sad makeup stash. "Can you work with that?"

She clucks. "No. I'll be back. Dry your hair while I'm gone. Brush it. Naturally. I'll get my rollers while I'm getting the makeup."

Thirty minutes later, I'm in rollers, the metal hooks burning my earlobes, and Tima blots my red lipstick and then smoothes on shiny gloss. When she steps out of the way, I blink, not recognizing myself with the bright blue eyeshadow on my lids and thick mascara on my lashes. Bright blush draws drastic lines up my cheeks. It's probably not as dark as many wear, but it looks out of place on me. New.

"A masterpiece," Tima says, stepping back and unrolling the first few rollers as I stare open-mouthed at my reflection.

She uncoils all the rest of the rollers on my head, and my hair bounces around me in beautiful waves. Even my hair is in on the fun because I swear it shines like it hasn't in my entire life. It's like my hair woke up and said, "New year, new me." It feathers perfectly when Tima runs a brush through it. Even my damn hair behaves like it's scared I'll never fix it again if it sags or looks dull.

I look like Tima and the friends she hangs out with. Not a soul from my school job would recognize me, and I smile at the fact that I don't care what they think now. I can go to any bar I please. I signed a character contract when I was hired that kept me out of bars and pool halls. It kept me from drinking, cigarettes, and men while not married.

But I am under no contract tonight.

Turn the Beat

Nicole

The man at the door is built like a brick shithouse and looks me up and down with such a sneer that I shrink behind Tima and her friend. Miriam Price is so beautiful that I surely look like the stepsister who wears hand-me-downs to the ball as I practically whimper behind her blonde hair and minidress.

To my surprise, the bouncer nods. Both women with me smile at the bouncer, and Tima grabs my hand, leading me through the door.

I've never been in a place like this. It's beyond my wildest imagination, and I squint as my eyes adjust to the light. And...there's *a lot* of light.

Purple and white shimmers come off the disco ball above us. The dance floor, lit in purple and blue neon lights and raised in the center of the room, gives the impression of a boxing ring as patrons gather around the base of it. Two bars, one on each side of the room, offer drinks. One of the bars is dedicated to beer and wine, the other to hard liquor and mixed cocktails.

Next to me, Miriam and Tima both wiggle their butts and bump hips in time to the music, laughing. The fringe around Tima's top shakes wildly and draws all eyes to her cleavage. Eventually, Tima notices I'm not engaged in the celebration of a night out and straightens her face. "Close your mouth. You look like you're catching flies. Go to the bar and get a drink. It'll make you feel better."

I glance at the bar, confused. "I've never ordered a drink at a bar. What do I do?"

Wrong thing to say.

"I can't help you," she says, and I hear the disappointment in her voice. "We'll be over in the booth with those guys." She points to a booth behind the dance floor. I smile a little because I'm pretty sure Tima and Miriam aren't fitting in that booth with eight men and another woman already in it and gathered around something on the table in front of them.

Tima and Miriam walk off, and I make a beeline for the bar. I may not be a big drinker, but drugs scare me to death. If I have to choose a chemical here, I'll go with alcohol. Besides, Tima said something about a Soviet drink I should try.

I approach the crowded bar and quietly try to hide and get a drink at the same time, which won't work. People around me wave dollar bills in the air and yell things at the bartenders waiting on them. The music is loud, so I can't hear much beyond the people directly in front of me ordering their drinks. A woman a few people over leans across the bar and pulls her shirt down, licking her lips at the male bartender until he slides over to serve her. I look down at my halter top. Yeah, there's no way I can pull this down without my boobs coming out entirely.

"You have to get in there. Don't be shy," a voice says next to my ear, startling me.

"Is it that obvious I'm not a big bar person?" I ask, turning to the man who just spoke to me.

Dear. Sweet. Lord. Christ. Jesus.

My eyes move over the man, and my stomach drops like I'm in a runaway elevator. He's a couple inches taller than an average man, but he leans down to make eye contact at my level. His hair is somewhere between long and short and curls nicely at his neck except for some curls that he's tamed around his forehead. His hair is dark, and he sports a perfectly trimmed, dark mustache I want to smooth with my index fingers because he looks so much like that actor who was in that car movie, albeit a bit younger. His brown eyes are the most magical I've ever seen. Granted, that could be because the disco ball's light shimmers over his face. He smiles, showing perfectly white teeth that are mildly crowded around the canines like my own.

I guess him to be about thirty-five, maybe a year or two older, and a quick perusal of the length of his body tells me he's a fashionable dresser. This is a man who cares how he looks. I can imagine him lint brushing his black shirt which is open a few buttons and showing a smattering of chest hair. The amount of dark hair is so perfect – not enough to be obnoxious, but enough to tell me he's well past puberty.

"Did you need help then?" he asks, tilting his head to the side and studying my face.

I wonder what he sees. Can he tell this outfit is borrowed? That my hair probably doesn't get this feathered on a normal night?

What would Tima do? What would Tima do? I chant the question in my head as I throw my head back to position my hair perfectly and smile the biggest smile I can. She'd flirt with him.

"I'm a little shy. Do I just push through?"

"With that top? You could just shimmy through that line of men over there and get pretty much whatever you want. Dex Holden," he says, holding out his hand. "Let me help you."

"I'm Nicole. OK, Dex. I'll have a white communist."

He squints, and his lips move into a smirk. "What?"

"Um, I may have got that wrong. White...Russian? Do they have those here?"

He laughs. He actually freaking laughs, and it's so beautiful – so engrossing – that I'm not mad that he's laughing at my expense. I wring my hands, wondering what to do next now that I've obviously turned him off. I jolt in surprise when his warm hand is suddenly on my lower back.

"That was a good one," he says, shaking his finger at me. "I'll have to remember it. You're funny." He pushes me forward a bit as he nudges us both up to the crowded bar.

The man next to him sneers at the intrusion but soon takes a step back when he sees Dex. "Sorry, Mr. Holden," the man says, holding up his hands like he's being robbed. He moves further down the bar, and Dex and I lean comfortably against the wood.

Dex raises his hand to get the bartender's attention. Other hands are raised near us, tits are out, and some patrons even wave *large* bills at the two bartenders working. To my surprise, the bartender approaches Dex immediately. "What can I get you, Mr. Holden?"

Is Dex someone important here?

"Do you own this place?" I ask.

Dex smiles and orders our drinks at the same time he slides a ten-dollar bill across the bar, telling the bartender to keep it. When the bartender leaves, Dex turns to me and casually leans on the bar like he *does* own the place. "Not yet, sweetheart. Owners don't usually pay for drinks," he says with a smile. "But I'm well-respected, and I tip well. Why are you here?"

I jerk my head in the direction Tima walked. "My roommate dragged me out. I got fired today. I guess this is her attempt to cheer me up."

The bartender appears with my drink and a martini for Dex, and I stare at the beige concoction in front of me.

"You've never had one of those before, huh?" Dex asks.

I shake my head. "I'm kind of a drinking virgin except for a few sips of wine."

Dex leans closer to me. "Well, let's pop that cherry, shall we?" He whispers it in my ear, and I shiver as his breath moves over my lobe and down my neck. It's suddenly very warm in the club, and I'm hyper-aware of the sensory experiences around me. The lights move over every surface of the room, and the music switches to a faster song.

He clinks his martini glass with my white Russian and downs half his drink in one go. Pulling the olive out of the glass, he sucks it off the toothpick and focuses back on me. I've never held the attention of a man like this before, and I've certainly never had the attention of a man like *him*.

"Why'd you get fired? Fuck a coworker?" He waggles his eyebrows.

"Why does everyone keep asking me that?"

"Do you have a reputation?" he asks, but there's laughter in his voice. He's teasing me.

"That's the funny thing about it. I certainly don't." I taste my drink, barely sipping it, and immediately put it back down. Ew.

"Don't like alcohol either, huh?" Dex says, picking up my glass and swirling the creamy liquid. "I better taste it to make sure Robbie made it right." Tilting the glass, he swallows a large gulp of my abandoned cocktail. He smacks his lips for a moment and then waves the bartender over again by only waggling two fingers.

"Is something wrong, Mr. Holden?" the bartender asks.

"Nothing is wrong. Can you get this beautiful woman a Shirley Temple?"

The bartender nods and walks away. "What's a Shirley Temple?" I ask. My fingers itch to wave down the bartender and tell him I'm fine. The drink is fine. I don't like making waves, and I don't want him to make me a different drink.

Dex laughs and rubs his face. "You really don't get out much, do you? Relax, it's a virgin drink." He stares at me a moment. "I think you'll like it. I know I like the occasional virgin...drink." Heat moves up my neck and to my cheeks. "Now, tell me why you got canned. I'm very interested in hearing this story." He sets his martini down, and I'm mesmerized by the purple light bouncing off the clear fluid.

I blink, trying to think and not look at every little detail about anyone and anything around me. "They said I needed to go to church more."

"Jesus Christ." Dex's eyes widen like he's never heard such a thing. He probably hasn't. It's clear we come from two different worlds.

"Literally," I mumble. He probably can't hear me over the loud music. I lean forward and speak next to his ear, and he puts his hand gently at my waist. I've seen men do this with Tima and Miriam, but never to me. I stumble a little, but his hand at my waist keeps me upright. "I worked at a religious grade school."

He gives a short nod and a smile. "Well, that's some shit, huh?"

The bartender brings my drink and sets it in front of Dex. Not me. The man slings his white bar rag over his shoulder and nods at Dex in a show of respect. The bartender doesn't move to the next customer, breathe, or smile until Dex approves the drink.

"Are you sure you're not the owner? If not the owner, are you the manager?" I ask.

"Neither." He slides the drink to me after it meets his approval. "Maybe someday," he says, sighing. "I own my own dance studio a few blocks away. I find talent here. They know me."

"Talent? What kind of talent?"

"Dancers mostly. I need teachers or demonstrators. I find people who can dance, pay them a few bucks to show my classes some moves, and everyone's happy."

"What kind of dance?" My eyes dart around the room. Modern styles, I'm certain.

"Disco mostly, but I teach a little of everything. I even teach jazz and tap classes for children. Those have a waitlist a mile long and fill up fast. Everyone wants their little Suzy to learn jazz." He rolls his eyes. "Even more annoying are the old people who are trying to relive their youth. Learning the Hustle is the midlife crisis of the Midwest. You understand?"

"I think so."

"You've never heard of Holden School of Dance?"

"I don't get out much," I say.

"Not to places like this, huh?" Dex asks, taking a sip of my old drink.

I look around again, and a small smile slides up one side of my mouth. A smirk, really. "No, I mean anywhere. I don't get out."

"That seems a waste. You're beautiful." Dex smiles again.

A blush creeps up my neck. Thankfully, Dex probably won't notice with the bar lighting.

"Will you dance with me?" he asks, sliding his hand up from my waist and trailing his fingers over my arm.

I open my mouth to speak, but nothing comes out. Laughter replaces my words, and I snort. Awkwardly. Taking a drink of my Shirley Temple – which is quite good – I stall, my mind frantically looking for an excuse not to make a damn fool of myself. "I don't know how. I'm just here for a drink."

"You're not even really drinking," Dex says. "Come dance with me. One song. I need to get up there anyway. Find some fresh talent. You never know when you'll find the next instructor or big thing."

"My only experience with this type of dancing is TV."

Dex puts his finger under my chin and tilts my face to look into those damnable brown eyes. A dimple creeps into one of his cheeks. "Then you're already as much of a professional as every other person in here."

Before I can argue, my feet move. Dex leads me to the dance floor. Actually, Dex pushes me to the dance floor if pushing can be done in a sexy and gentle way. After meeting him, I can confirm it can. This is interesting and something I should talk to Tima about. Then again, she probably already knows. There's something scintillating about having him behind me and walking toward a new experience with a sexy man mere inches from my back.

He leads me up the dance floor stairs, and I look around, obviously out of place as everyone gives me a weird look. I don't blame them. I'm on the dance floor and not moving.

Dex is suddenly in front of me. "The key to disco is always staying on beat but not letting yourself get too tired. This goes on for hours." He looks my body up and down. "You look scared."

"I am scared."

"Why?" he asks.

I look around again and can feel the panicked creases on my forehead. "I'm on a dance floor in my new city, I just lost my job, and the guy in front of me is gorgeous. I'm a little nervous, OK?"

Dex bites his bottom lip, then licks it as he shakes his shoulders. He moves his face until it's two inches from my own. "You think I'm gorgeous?" We stare at each other a moment until he clears his throat. "Do what I do. You'll be fine. Be my mirror image."

Dex moves side to side with a bounce in his step. He puts his hands on my hips and makes me move with him. I look around, and he tilts my chin to him again, forcing me to look at his face. "Look at me. Not at them. They may look, but they don't care. Trust me. Even if they do, do *you* care?"

"We haven't met. My name is Nicole Tate, and I'm a people pleaser."

"A people pleaser, huh?" He smirks. "I like to please people, too." Was that a sexual innuendo? "But don't worry about pleasing these people. If you're...performing with a partner, you focus on them. I'm the only person in the room you care about right now."

I look into his eyes and notice goldish halos in the irises. They practically sparkle in the disco ball light. Reflective sparks of color from my halter top move over his face and body. His hands guide me, and I'm soon stepping and matching him. My arms are stiff at my sides because I'm not sure what to do with them.

He notices and runs his hands down my arms, making every single micro hair on my body stand on end. My nipples harden in my top, which is a new feeling for me. I understand now, though. I understand why Tima and Miriam traipse off to the club every weekend. This male attention is something I've never had, and my head spins like I'm drunk off it.

"What do I do with my hands?" I ask.

He smiles a devilish grin and leans toward me. "Never ask a man that question if you're not ready for it, Nicole."

It's not the first time he's been close tonight, but it's the first time I notice that he smells good. Really damn good. Like a man. A hint of sweat is somewhere beneath faint laundry detergent and a light cologne. It's not overwhelming like some men spray. He's aware of what he's wearing and knows damn well that an overpowering scent in a club would turn people off.

But he also knows that a woman up close would find the scent arousing. Like it's only for her.

His hands slide down to my wrist and then away again to do his own hand movements, which are small and loose. Nothing huge. No large pointer fingers. It's subtle, and I remember what he said about disco being an experience that goes on for the whole night. The movements are liquid, and he moves his hips and shoulders in a relaxed way I try to emulate.

I shimmy my shoulders in a swivel motion until I feel like I'm somewhat matching him. I'm aware that eyes are watching Dex. I'm happy they're not watching me, but I don't like the other women watching him like they wish he was dancing with them and I'm not good enough. Something possessive comes over me, lighting a fire under my ass.

I *have* to impress this man.

I spy Tima in my peripheral vision as she sashays onto the dance floor with Miriam. When she sees me with Dex, she stops short and opens her mouth in surprise. If Tima is shocked, Miriam looks positively scandalized that I managed to land the hottest and best dancer in the place. She scowls, and her lips turn into a sneer. I expect no support or cheering from her because she's Tima's friend, but her expression reminds me of the pithy jealousy women have for other females.

I flick my eyes back to Dex, focusing on the man in front of me like he asked. Soon, I'm smiling as my hips and knees loosen up. I may not be perfect, but I'm moving like the people around me. Dex is a dance instructor and does this for a living. He's expected to be good.

I squeeze my eyes shut for a few moments and dance. I let myself go and do what my body feels like doing. A freedom I've never felt before moves from my feet into my body as the beat vibrates the dance floor. I can feel the music and the people dancing nearby. The air between Dex and my breasts practically crackles with electricity.

When I open my eyes, Tima and Miriam are gone. Searching the room to see if they've left me here, I eventually spot them in a nearby booth with two men bent over a white substance. Tima smiles at me, but Miriam leans over the drugs on the table so I can't see her face. I blink twice, suddenly scared that I'm in the same room as drugs, and Dex notices.

He follows my line of sight. "You don't do drugs?"

I shake my head. "Never tried them." I look back at him. "Do you do drugs? Are you going to push them on me?"

Laughter erupts from his mouth and people nearby stop and stare as the music around us changes to a new song. "Yeah, sweetheart, I'm going to get my trench coat and jump out from around the back dumpster. 'Hey, baby, I got some good powder.' What do I look like?"

"Trouble!" I yell over the music. "You look like trouble to me. Everything I've ever been warned about in life is either in this room or standing right in front of me."

He smiles and moves closer to me until we're touching as we move in unison. My entire body tingles, my stomach trembles, and a line of nervous sweat drips down my spine. "I *am* trouble," he says. "But to answer your question, I don't fuck with cocaine. Not my thing. Now some quaaludes to calm the nerves every now and then? You've really never even tried it?"

"No, and I won't."

"Noted. Doesn't mean we can't be friends." A slower song comes on, and I awkwardly step back from Dex. "Want another Shirley Temple?" he asks.

Why is this guy still hanging out with me? A quick look around shows there are two hundred beautiful women in the room, most of whom are probably salivating over Dex Holden. But he follows me to the bar where he raises his hand yet again and summons the bartender like a king. He doesn't even speak to Robbie this time – just makes a hand gesture between us.

"Where are you going to work now that you're without a job?" he asks out of the blue.

I shake my head. "I don't know. I haven't thought that far." I prop my head in my hands and lean forward until my hair flops into my face. I feel sorry for myself for a few seconds until I remember where I am. People don't want to see a sad woman at the disco. I raise my head and blow my bangs out of my eyes. "I'm kind of licking my wounds here, but I'll need to think about it tomorrow. Bills will be due the end of the month."

"Sounds like you need a job interview," Dex says, casually leaning against the bar. A drop of sweat rolls down his temple, and my fingers itch to swipe it away.

"Do you know of one?" I ask, chuckling and taking a drink of my Shirley Temple as soon as the bartender sets it in front of me.

"We can talk at home."

"Excuse me?" I ask, practically spitting out my drink. I pound on my chest to keep from choking. "Home?"

He throws back his martini like it's water and sucks the pimento out of his olive before answering. He holds out his hand for me and straightens to his full height. "We should hash out the details somewhere quieter. My place isn't far from here."

Wild

Dex

I can practically smell the innocence on her. It smells like a perfume she obviously borrowed from that roommate of hers. It doesn't fit her skin. Even if she hadn't told me, I'd know she's as pure as the driven snow. It's in the way she walks and the way she looks at things with big eyes. She moves through the world like she's never seen anything on the planet before.

I'm fucking captivated by it.

I also knew she'd be perfect for my plan when I saw her. I can mold her. Teach her how to move. The judges will love her, but I need to gain her trust before I spring that on her. Giving her a job will give her a reason to trust me, and it'll give me an opportunity to know her better.

It's been years since I met a woman like her. She doesn't fawn over me like she knows exactly who I am. I'm a hot member of the club scene and have been for years. The same women, night after night and year after year, ask me to take them home and fuck them or bring Felix over for us both to have a go.

This woman doesn't know me. She doesn't know liquor and quaaludes. She doesn't know the unspoken club rules on how to ignore people beneath you and buy drinks and cocaine for the people you see as above you – people who can give you things, whether it's sex, drugs, or even a role in a play or car dealership commercial.

When was the last time I had someone in the palm of my hand who is so kind, so wide-eyed and fresh? She's honest and hard-working. I can tell by the way she's disappointed she lost her job. It stings her pride. Where there's pride in work, there's a hard worker. I need a hard worker, and I need a dance partner.

She came to my house, following me like a lost puppy. How many women would do that with someone they don't know, especially with that serial killer on the loose who lures women to his car by asking for help? She's trusting. Hopeful.

And something deep in my gut and even lower in my balls doesn't want to let her down. That's interesting because I've certainly let down my fair share of women over the years. I haven't given two shits about them beyond what they could do for me or how good they could fuck. The women who aren't into it usually get one look at my relationship with Felix and head for the hills, calling me every sick name in the book as they go, usually after they've fucked both of us. I'm used to it because sharing isn't for everyone.

I push my bronze key into the lock of my apartment door and turn the knob. "We haven't cleaned for a few days. Sorry about any mess. I can't remember what it looked like when I left."

She tilts her head and blinks. God, that innocent fucking expression is just too much. "Who's we?"

"My roommate. Felix. You have a roommate, right? What's her name?"

"Tima."

I snap my fingers. "You should have brought her."

"Did you want to interview her too?"

"Does she need a job?" I ask.

Nicole shakes her head, the soft curls bouncing with her. Unable to stop myself, I push one of the curls behind her ear.

"I just thought men of your age don't usually have roommates."

I ignore the comment because I don't know how to reply since Felix and I are way more than roommates. Swinging the door open, I wave her into the apartment. Looking around, I take in my living room with fresh eyes, trying to imagine how she sees it for the first time. Our top-of-the-line TV is on a TV cart in the corner, a plaid couch sits in the middle of the room, and a luxurious black swivel chair in a modern style is off to the side. Everything is in dark colors in respect of Felix's disgust for anything bright yellow or orange. I gesture towards the chair and shut the door. Maybe if she feels welcome, she'll stay.

"Would you like some water or coffee?" I ask. "I always like it when people offer me one of those after a club night."

"Do you go every night?"

I sit down on the plaid couch across from her as she slowly lowers herself into the black chair. "Not every night, but I'm usually there a couple times a week. Like I said, it's a good place to find talent. I can't have a disco class at the studio without someone who knows how to do it and will show new moves. I find seasonal teachers that way. If I have guest instructors, I don't have to teach every class, and my students get variety."

Nicole clears her throat and crosses her arms in front of her chest. She looks down at her cleavage, and I wonder if she feels self-conscious about her top now that she's not in the club and is sitting in a normal living room. "You said something about a job for me. Maybe you should explain some details about what I'd be doing. You've seen me dance and surely can't imply you want me as a dance teacher."

"My front desk assistant just had a baby, and she's not coming back. We need someone to run the office, answer the phone, do the payroll for the instructors, sign up new students, and accept the checks and cash people bring to pay for lessons. How are you at bookkeeping?"

A blank look crosses her face, and her eyes flick to something behind me. Her hands wring in her lap. "I've never done it, but I entered grades into a little grade book with lines. Is it like that?"

"Close enough," I say, as a scuffling sound comes from one of the back bedrooms. Nicole looks up just as a rumpled Felix saunters into the room wiping sleep from his eyes. "Ah, here's

Felix. Roommate and co-worker. He's my head dance instruc-tor. Full staff member. I consider him a…partner, though."

Felix blinks twice and shakes his head a little as Nicole's mouth drops open. I don't blame her. My mouth still drops open when I see him.

His short hair is rumpled from sleep, and he's clean-shaven, unusual for our circle of friends with their mustaches and mut-ton chops. I run my fingers over my own mustache as I think about it. I like him with a little stubble, though. I like running my fingers over it when he sucks me off. There's such a differ-ence between a man with a hard jaw and stubble doing that and a soft-skinned woman doing it. Both are nice, and I'm a true believer that variety is the spice of life.

Felix runs one hand down the front of his purple, silk pajama shirt and holds the other out to Nicole. They nod at each other, Nicole still too shell-shocked by Felix's appearance in my living room to do more than close her open mouth.

"Felix, this is Nicole…" My voice trails off when I realize I suddenly can't remember this creature's last name. It must have been the pills I took before I met her combined with the martinis. I'll need to be sure not to take anything around her since she doesn't like it.

"Tate." She says the word with a husky voice. I know that voice. It's the voice of a woman who sees something she likes.

"Felix Rathbone," Felix says, taking Nicole's hand and press-ing a kiss to it. This is his normal routine. I may bring a woman – or man- home, and Felix flirts and seduces along with me. We may have startled him from a deep sleep, but he knows his role well.

I'm just not sure if I want this woman to be a standard routine for us. She doesn't seem like the type you kick out as soon as the cum rag hits the floor. There's something about her I want to...keep.

The word rattles around in my brain as I think it. In the past, fear reared its ugly head whenever I thought about keeping someone beyond Felix. He's my best friend. My lover. He's been with me for years now – so long that I don't even remember how it started unless I concentrate. We melted into each other like butter and chocolate while everyone else in my life was like oil and water. There were women in my early twenties I thought I should "keep," but they never stayed, and I eventually stopped thinking I'd ever have the traditional marriage with a woman. It's something I've wanted deep down for so long that it hurts to think about. I've pushed that desire down into the abyss of my soul, and I've dulled myself with love for Felix. Felix is safe. Routine. But it's not like I can legally marry a man. There's also more to it than that. I want a family. I also dream of more than just the quietness of sitting across one person for the rest of my life. I want a full table of love and partnership in my life. I always have.

"Please sit," Felix says, jolting me from my thoughts.

Felix joins me on the couch, his thigh touching mine. Nicole notices the proximity, and her eyes track the several inches of cushion space on either side of us. It's obvious we're together, and it's almost funny to watch her expression as she realizes it.

Her eyebrows raise so high I can't see them for her bangs. Her mouth opens in a little O formation, and she puts her hands in her lap, squeezing and unsqueezing the fabric of her pants. "Are you two gay men?"

The words leave her mouth before she catches them with the hand that claps over her mouth. Her eyes widen to the size of tea plates, and I lean forward.

"I'm sorry," she says, shaking her head before I can speak. "It's just not something I'm used to." She breaks my eye contact and looks around our room. She idly plays with the glass candy dish holding the butterscotch candies Felix likes. "I'm from downstate. That stuff is unheard of. I know it's common around Chicago, but I've been in my own world and worked at a religious institution..."

"Relax, Nicole." I hold my hands up, trying to soothe her like she's a crazed horse. "We're not gay."

She looks back at me. "You're not?" She moves her index finger, pointing. "I've never seen straight men sit so close."

"We're bisexual," Felix says.

"What's that? Is that a new word?"

"Actually, it is. I mean, people like us have always been around since the start of human history, but it's only recently that there's been a term for it," I explain. "It means we like both men and women."

Nicole's face pales. "Both? You sleep with both men and women?"

"Yes. Sleep and date, if we ever find the right person. We want to expand our relationship to include someone else we fall in love with," I explain.

"We don't discriminate against anyone," Felix says, his voice heavy with want. I need to calm him down before he scares the sweet woman. "We're equal opportunity fuckers."

Too late.

Heat builds in Nicole. Even I can see it from a few feet away. Her exposed chest and shoulders turn red, and the color creeps into her cheeks. "Maybe I'm in the wrong place," she whispers. "I don't know if I'll fit in with you gentlemen."

"Gentlemen?" Felix chuckles next to me. "She really is in the wrong place if she thinks we're gentlemen."

I tilt my head and smile at her, trying to reassure her and ignoring Felix. "Why did you come home with me tonight, Nicole?"

"You said you had a job for me. I need a job."

"I do have a job for you. But I could have interviewed you at the studio tomorrow. Do you trust me?"

"Oddly, yes. Even though I've been told not to trust strange men, I figured there wasn't any harm since everyone at the club knows you and saw me leave with you. I guess..." She stops suddenly and looks out our square window over the back of the couch, probably admiring the Chicago skyline. Felix, for his part, wisely shuts the fuck up.

"You guess what?" I ask, desperately wanting to show her I'm listening. I want to know what she says. What she thinks.

"I guess I wanted to be wild, you know? I had a really, really bad day. I don't use bad words often, but it was shit. I had a shitty day. Shit, shit, shit, shit, and then more shit. My roommate dressed me tonight because I'm usually a square." She looks back at me. "And you're so handsome and suave. The whole club bent over backward to talk to you. I guess I wanted to feel wild and wanted for one damn night of my life." She looks down at the floor, and I swear I see her eyes fill with tears. "But I don't have the horsepower for two men. There is no way I'm special enough for that."

Even if Felix doesn't give two shits about this woman, he cocks his head to the side to listen. He's fascinated. His silence and the fact he's letting me handle the situation is damning. He knows I like her. At this point, he's going to let me take the lead. He sinks back into the couch where I know he'll stay until I ask him to move.

I crawl across the floor on my knees and grab her hands. "First, you are special. Any man would be happy to be with you and give you the wildest night of your life." She blinks, and a tear slides down her face. "Is that why you came home with me?"

She nods. "God, I feel so awkward." She looks away like she can't meet my eyes. "But now I'm just scared. Scared and stupid."

My hand slides over her knees. She jolts at the touch but allows it. I study her face and notice the pulse in her throat. It's fast, and I'm sure I'm unsettling her. "Nicole, what were you expecting from me here tonight?"

"I don't want to say," she says, squeezing her eyes shut and shaking her head like a child.

"Did you want to have sex with me?"

"I wanted the job you said you had, and I wanted to be wild, you know? If that means sex, then yes. But I'm not sure anymore, and now I hear myself sounding like a tease girl my mother warned me about being..."

"Stop," I say when her voice trails off. She looks at me again and blinks like she's never been told to stop talking before. "We don't have to have sex, and I still have a job for you. I'm sorry my relationship with Felix is awkward for you, but I kind of like him."

Her eyes flick to Felix. "I can see why."

She doesn't move my hands off her knees. Instead, she places her hands on top of mine. Her face changes at the action, her cheeks softening. I watch her hands trace around my fingers.

"Nicole," I whisper. "You said you came here to be wild. Do you still want to be?"

Felix scoots to the edge of the sofa behind me. He inhales through his nose and then stops breathing like he's waiting for me to set an itinerary on how we're going to seduce the beautiful virgin that's dropped into our laps.

Nicole looks at me, and her knees tremble a little under my hands like she's cold. "Y-yes," she stammers. "I don't want to have sex since it would be my first time. I'm not s-sure I'm ready for that. B-but maybe a kiss?"

I slide my hands up her thighs. "There are other ways to be wild besides kissing and sex. There are lines between those two things."

She cocks her head and furrows her brow. "Like what?"

"Dear, Lord," Felix practically swoons behind me.

"Would you like me to show you?" I ask, ignoring Felix. He can watch. He's done it before.

"Wh-what is it?" She's back to stammering, and the shaking of her voice and knees is now spreading to her entire body. The chair vibrates with her fear and nerves, but her eyes are dark, and she licks her lips. She's like a scared rabbit but also like a ravenous, sexually deprived housewife.

"Have you ever had anyone touch you...here?"

I run my hand up her leg and lazily run my thumb over the crotch of her pants like it's no big deal. She startles but quickly corrects herself. She wants to be touched. Everything about her is begging for it.

"No," she finally whispers.

"No one has ever touched you there, or you don't want me to?"

"I've never been touched there."

"Do you?" I nod at her center and smile at the slight wet line forming on the crotch of her pants. It's been a long time since I could make a woman soak both her pants and panties just for offering a hand job. "Do you touch yourself there?"

Her shoulders tense, and she looks at Felix, which only makes her lick her lips again. "I was taught not to. I was taught that was only for my husband, and good girls didn't do that."

My brows come together, and I tilt her chin to look at me. "I'm sorry they said that. Your body is not just for a husband's pleasure. Shit, it's 1978. I thought we were over that."

A trace of a smile lines her face. "I guess the small town where I'm from never got into the sexual revolution."

I can't control it any longer. This woman is going to experience her own sexual revolution right here in my living room. I'm going to touch her and even lick her until she's a sobbing, whimpering mess on my chair.

Felix is on board. I know because we have a silent way of communicating. It's practically telepathic. He scoots back again and gives me room. Instinctually, we both know she'll only tolerate one man in her space right now.

I grip Nicole's hips and watch surprise cross her face as I pull her down so she's right at the edge of the chair. I don't break eye contact. She needs that. I know she does. "I'm going to unbutton your pants and slide them down. Then, I'm going to take off your panties. Is that OK?"

She doesn't answer, but I take the fact that she gives a short nod as a yes. My fingers whisper over the button of the purple pants, and I unzip them slowly, letting her enjoy every sound. I want her to remember this as a positive experience. I want her to play it in her head when she's an old lady on her seventieth birthday.

When everything is unbuttoned and unzipped, I hook my fingers inside the waistband and slide them down her strong, beautiful legs inch by fucking inch until she's so desperate to get them off herself when they hit her ankles that she kicks them aside.

She's not wearing any panties, and her modesty kicks in as soon as her pants hit the carpet. She cups herself with her hands like she's suddenly realized she's naked from the waist down. I kneel between her legs, my hands on her thighs, rubbing her skin and trying to comfort her and warm her since the air is cool.

I slowly move my hands higher. "I know you're shy, so I'm going to use your own finger to touch you."

"Wh-what?"

"Put your middle finger right at the top of your slit. I'm going to show you how to do this so you don't need us. I mean, it's nice to be needed every once in a while, but let me teach you how to do this for yourself."

She takes a deep breath and does what I ask. Her finger trembles over her clit, but she bites her lip at her own touch. I position her finger until it's exactly over where it needs to be. I'm so angry for this woman that I want to put my fist through my own wall. She doesn't even know where her own clit is. I realize I live in a world where I'm free and most people I know are free, but Nicole seems so repressed - so pushed down by whoever told her she couldn't touch her own pussy.

I press my thumb firmly over her finger and move it in circles. "Put your head back on the chair, close your eyes for me, and enjoy this, Nicole. I'll help you."

She looks at me like she doesn't want to take her eyes off me, but then she does what I say. I place a small kiss on her leg, and she gasps. I'm close enough to smell the earthiness of her and feel the heat of her center as I press our fingers down further on her clit. A small squeak comes from her mouth. "Like that?" I ask, looking for validation she's having a good time.

"Yes," she says, the words practically a whisper.

I use firm pressure for a few circles and then back off until her finger whispers across her slit for a few seconds. The back and forth of it is driving her insane as her thighs tighten against me, and my innocent virgin bucks into my hand.

I know women, and I know she's about a minute away from experiencing her first orgasm. I place another kiss on her knee and drag my tongue up her leg. "When you come, you'll shake and your toes will curl because it's so good. Has anyone told you what to expect?"

"N-no," she says.

"It'll feel good with my hand, but it'll be so much better if you let me do it with my tongue."

She jolts up so fast that my hand loses its grip on her. She sits up wide-eyed. "Your mouth? On my..." She waves her hand over her pussy area. I'm still between her legs, and I avert my eyes to her slit. It's wet with want, just waiting for me to put my mouth over her engorged clit and suck. "You can do that?"

Fuck, I want to teach her everything.

I place my hand on her abdomen and push her back. Without a word to make her more uncertain, I trail my tongue further up her leg until I'm hovering over her clit. I breathe on it for a second. She doesn't push me away, so I drop one small kiss on it.

Her hands come to my shoulders, and she squeezes my shirt like she's in a runaway train car. Her legs spread wide, and I take that as my cue to go to town on her. I lap. I lick the salt off every part I can reach – the creases, the nub that practically trembles under my tongue, and the hole that's warm and inviting. I slide the tip of my tongue inside her pussy and swirl it, tasting something savory that reminds me of dinner.

When I've had my fill of tasting her pussy, I flick my tongue over her clit again and laugh as she grips my hair. When I attempt to move away from her, she tilts her pelvis and grinds against me. "Dex," she breathes, and I reach into my pants to caress my dick.

Felix can take care of that later, though. Tonight is about Nicole – making her feel welcome and teaching her how a man can make her feel.

She breaks apart while I'm consumed with my own thoughts, but there's no denying the orgasm that tears through her. She moans a string of words I honestly didn't think she'd know, and she throws one of her legs over my shoulder. I run my hand up and down her leg as I hum my approval of her reaction.

When she's spent, I take a long lick up her entire pussy area and place a kiss under her belly button. "That's what they didn't want you to know."

"This makes sense now," she practically pants. "I know why women like it, and I know why my grandmother said any kind of hanky panky was only for my husband."

I place a kiss on her. "You believe that now?"

She looks down at me, still catching her breath. "No woman needs to get married if she can find someone who can do that."

Felix laughs behind me, and Nicole and I both startle. We both forgot he was there watching us. Nicole blushes again, but I look up at her and catch her chin in my hand. "Felix does it even better. Do you want another orgasm?"

Her eyes flick to Felix. "I can have another one? Two in one night?"

This woman. I laugh and move so that I'm standing over her. Kissing her forehead, I slowly move down her face until I kiss the tip of her nose. "You can have as many as you can handle. Or so I hear."

I look over my shoulder. "Felix, would you like to show our guest how good two orgasms in one night can be?"

Felix licks his lips and comes off the couch in a movement I can only describe as panther-like. He prowls over to her, never breaking eye contact and ready to pounce. He practically drools over the virgin I brought home to him like it's a leg of lamb, and his hand adjusts the hardening cock stretching the limits of his pajama pants.

I know he'll give me what I need later, and I'll certainly have fun taking care of that cock later, too.

Felix smiles the evil grin that made me fall in love with him. It's a dangerous smirk and the one he uses when he wants the world to know that he's going to make someone lose their shit.

I gently pull Nicole out of her seat and turn her so I'm behind her. "Sit on my lap and let Felix have a lick."

I sink into the vacated chair and pull her with me before she can answer. She lets me control her body. She's like the gelatin molds I've seen housewives make – quivering and pliable.

"He won't hurt you," I coo into her ear. "Quite the opposite, really. Close your eyes and lean back on me. You want to enjoy him like other women have. They've had no complaints."

Something about my comment about other women loving what Felix does with his mouth does it. Is she looking for validation? Sexual adventure she's never had before but other women have clamored for? She practically melts like butter into my torso, and I'm brazen enough to slide my fingers down her halter top, pulling her breasts out and flicking her nipples. They harden immediately, and her ass cheeks tense under me.

"Open your eyes and watch Felix eat your pussy."

I wrap my arms around her harder, pulling her closer. As if that's possible. It's the only thing I can think of to stop her trembling. She shakes so hard I worry she'll bite her tongue.

But something about her fear turns me on. She's afraid and titillated about what Felix will do with his dangerous smile.

He does what I did, but he does it a thousand times better. His mouth is everywhere, and he cares nothing about being kind. This is about him being able to taste what he wants. And right now, he wants this woman's full bush in his face and his cheeks covered with her want. He spits on her, watching the drool run down to her asshole just so he can catch it with his tongue and drag it over every inch of her slit. He sucks. He licks. He forcefully holds her legs apart when she instinctually tries to shut them because she's ashamed of how much she likes his ravaging mouth. He closes his eyes in fucking rapture as he tastes my spit mixed with her pleasure all over her skin.

I palm her breasts and kiss her neck. Eventually, my hand comes gently to her throat, and I hold it there until she screams so loud from the pleasure that I'll expect an eviction notice on my door tomorrow.

Help Wanted

Nicole

"Let me understand this bullshit," Tima says, wrapping her smiling lips around a thin cigarette and inhaling deeply. She blows the smoke out before continuing. "You went home with the hot guy from the disco, met his roommate, and you let them go down on you? *Both* of them?"

I tap my hands on the table. "It was a job interview." I hear how ridiculous it sounds when I say it, but it's the only thing I can say to rationalize what happened.

"Honey, that's not like any job interview I've ever heard of." She stubs her cigarette out in our little brown ashtray she likely stole from the local bowling alley. "If there's a job interview like that, it usually involves the woman being the one on her knees. What was it like?" she asks, sniffing.

My eyebrows move to my hairline. "You've never had that done to you before? Here I thought I was behind in never having that done for me."

Tima sputters a laugh. "I've had it done. Just not by *two* guys. Not sure how you roped that horse on your first rodeo."

I ignore her question and continue toweling off my wet hair, thinking. I've gone over last night in my head a million times. Who was I last night? I've never done anything like that. I've never gone home with a man, kissed a man like that, and let a man – let alone two of them- see any part of my body that's usually covered by underwear. To say nothing of me letting them put their mouths on me. I certainly never dreamed that was a thing. My mother never told me about any of this. Does she know about it? My friends back home never told me. Then again, most of my friends back home are virgins like me or are married. The married ones act like their underwear is nailed on. Birds of a feather flock together.

I've toyed with not going to the dance studio. I mean, do they really expect me to show up? Was it all just a ploy to get me into bed? Will they still want me now that I didn't deliver the full package and actually get in their bed?

It seems likely I was a night of fun. Fun for me, anyway. My face flushes with embarrassment at the idea I left them hanging. After I came, Felix kissed my leg one time before backing away. Dex kissed his way down my neck to my collarbone, probably wanting more to happen. But I thanked them like an idiot and walked out on wobbly legs. I had no idea what to do for them or even what to say. In fact, I think I did a funny salute before I shut the door. I can't remember, and the entire night is a blur.

The shrill ring of the telephone interrupts my thoughts, and Tima walks to the wall to pick up the phone. "Hi," she says casually, sure it's for her. It's probably Miriam. I never get phone calls.

Her brow furrows and she looks at me. Confused, she holds the phone out. "There's a guy asking for you."

I point to my chest and look behind me like there are other people in the kitchen with us. "Me?"

Tima covers the phone. "Did you give that guy your phone number?"

"No!" I whisper yell. "I pulled my pants and my halter top up and walked out of there like a dumbass." The image of Felix still wiping his mouth as I slid my feet into Tima's heels and grabbed my purse flashes through my memory.

"I think he found you."

"Damn telephone book. I knew I should have used my first initial instead of my full name."

"You gave him your full name? Your real one?" Tima asks. She clucks her tongue. "I have so much to teach you. Never give the full name. Fake is best."

She takes her hand off the receiver and puts the phone to her ear again. "Um, let me see if she's in. I can't locate her. Who is this, and what is this regarding?" she asks, her secretarial skills kicking in.

She's silent for a few moments, and I hear a low, rumbling voice through the phone all the way from the other side of the room. His voice is authoritative, even from several feet away.

"I see," Tima says. "Hold on." She covers the receiver again. "It's a gentleman named Dex, and he was wondering when you could come in and have him show you your desk and where everything is."

"He still wants me to work for him?"

Tima smiles and shimmies her shoulders. The bracelets on her wrist clink together. "I'd work for him if I'm going to get that kind of treatment."

I'm out of my chair and standing in front of Tima before I can think twice about it. She holds the phone out to me, and I hesitate. Can I work for a man who's seen me with my legs spread wide open? Tasted me?

"Rent is due next week," Tima says, her eyes boring into mine. She smiles a close-lipped grin as she hands me the phone.

I guess I can make an exception now that the financial consequences of not having a job are looking me in the face. Literally.

I take a deep breath and smile. Even though he can't see it, my mother told me to smile when I'm on the phone because a man can hear my smile.

I don't think Mom would survive in 1978. She's much better suited for 1950.

"Hello?" I ask, my voice husky. I clear my throat in the dead air. "Hello?" I ask again in case he didn't hear me.

"Hi, Nicole. Felix and I were wondering when you could come in. We need to teach you..." His voice trails off, and he sniffs on the other end. "We need to teach you your job."

"My job?" I ask like I'm an idiot - like I don't remember our entire employment conversation.

"The one I promised you," he says with a laugh. The laugh is low and kind. So kind. Wait. Are they actually nice men who live up to their end of the bargain? Do nice men perform what they did last night?

I need a job. Money is not optional in modern Chicago. I have rent. I have my half of the utilities. Hell, prices are through the roof, and I need my bus pass and groceries. Sure, I can live on tuna casserole, but what kind of life is that?

"Um, when should I come in?"

"Are you available now? I'm at the studio. We could talk before the next class. I have to teach a waltz class for middle-aged married couples who are trying to spice up their marriage at four."

I look at Tima, who is waving her hands and smiling. She obviously wants me to go and check it out.

Maybe this can be a good thing. It'll be money in my pocket, and it doesn't have to be forever. Just because we did what we did doesn't mean I can't act professionally. It's time to grow up. Women have slept with their bosses for years. Probably since the war. Hell, probably since the Iron Age or something. If he can be professional and provide me with a paycheck, I can show up and do my job for him.

I quickly write down the address Dex gives me over the phone and slide it into the back pocket of my jeans as I hang up the phone. He probably thinks I'm weird for not talking other than asking him for the address and telling him goodbye, but I can't dwell on that now.

I look down and lament my simple bell-bottom jeans and sweater belted at the waist. "Do I look OK for a job interview?" I ask Tima.

"Honey," she clucks and slides another cigarette out of the pack. I can already tell by the sound of her voice she's going to tell me I need extra help. "I don't think this is an interview. You already passed that last night. Go dry your hair and put some eyeshadow on, for fuck's sake. You got two hot bosses."

***

I take the bus downtown in record time and approach the non-descript building two blocks away from a stop. I expect a billboard with Dex's name on it or maybe a sign with a disco ball on it. Something colorful and fitting Dex's personality.

What I find is a simple sign with Dex's name and suite number on it and a blank, gray door with an unpolished handle.

I knock on the door, unsure if I can just walk in, and the door swings open before the third knock. Dex smiles at me with a confused smile, and I suddenly forget how to talk. I may feel awkward, but Dex Holden is gorgeous as hell.

"Um, I wasn't sure I could just walk in or if you were with clients," I say, jerking my finger over my shoulder. "Is this a good time?"

He chuckles and waves me in. "You don't have to knock. I suppose I should put something on the door that says to walk in. Besides, I invited you. Remember?"

I stare around the space, blinking. Inside, the building is a different world. There's a lobby with a bright yellow desk I assume will be mine. In the corner, there's a coffee percolator that's bubbling, probably in anticipation of Dex's waltz class, along with paper coffee mugs with cutout handles. A few avocado green chairs line the orange wallpapered wall, and a door off to the side has a picture of a dancing woman and man on it, obviously a single-stall bathroom anyone can use. Behind my work area are three doors. One looks like Dex's office with a desk in it. One has a mimeograph machine on a table, so it must be a supply room. The last door is closed. Across the room are large, pine double doors that probably lead to the dance area.

Dex claps his hands. "Let's show you around the place. We can start with the studio."

He places his hand on my lower back, and my legs tremble at his touch. He's touched me more personally than a simple hand on my back, but something about him touching me the day after licking my most intimate parts makes it feel even more scandalous.

"This is the dance area," he says proudly, swinging the double doors open.

If the lobby area was different from the outside of the build-ing, the inside of the studio practically makes me swoon. It looks like an entirely different world. Walking through the double doors into the studio is like Dorothy walking from black and white into color in *The Wizard of Oz*.

A large disco ball hangs from the vaulted ceiling. It spins, sadly not flashing any colorful light around since the overhead lights are on and drowning out any ambiance it would show. The dance floor is slightly raised with polished wood flooring. Mirrors surround the space, and a small music booth with an 8-track player and record player is across the room on a sturdy table.

I tentatively walk up the two steps to the dance floor and look around, mesmerized. I was at the club the other night with Dex, but he has his own club in a small dance studio. Shockingly, the two places could be twins.

"It's beautiful. This is all yours?" I ask.

Dex leans against the railing that surrounds the dance floor. "It's the only thing I ever wanted to do. I left school at sixteen when my mom kicked me out of the house."

"Why'd she kick you out?" I ask. I immediately bite my tongue. I shouldn't have asked such a personal question. It's not my business.

If Dex is peeved, he doesn't show it. He shrugs. "I had a girlfriend at the time. Mom spent a lot of time worried about having her in my bedroom. She should have been worried about the guy next door. Boy, was she surprised when she came home from the grocery store and came to my room to have me help her carry the groceries in." He looks in the mirror behind me and stares at his image. "I can still see the look on her face and hear the words she said to me." His eyes flick back to me. "Just so we're all clear here, having sex with men and women was unheard of and unacceptable in small-town Ohio in 1960."

I really shouldn't have asked his personal business. "I'm sorry," I say. "Not about you liking both men and women. I'm sorry about your mom. What did you do after you left?" I ask, hoping it's a happier part of the story.

"I lived on the streets of Cleveland for a couple of years, parking cars at upscale events and sleeping in the parking garages at night if it wasn't freezing. Over time, I became a club kid with some of the other runaways. This was the early sixties, so music and rebellion were just becoming a thing in the cities. Lots of kids were leaving households where they didn't fit – either through their own volition or their parents kicked them out," he says. "Anyway, I did that for several years – odd jobs during the day and dancing at the clubs at night. I'd find shared housing with ten other people and rotate sleep schedules." He looks down and shakes his head. "Looking back on it, it was wild. It was also crazy how we existed in the world without the so-called normal people ever knowing we were there and didn't have homes to call our own or even food."

I do the math in my head. I know Dex is older, but we never went through basic information last night. It seems silly for me to ask his age after he did what he did to me. I mentally run through the years and decide I was right about Dex being around thirty-five.

He sighs and looks at himself in the mirror again. "I came to Chicago on a weekend bus trip with some of the other kids. I couldn't even tell you their names, but I hope they're all OK. We clubbed the whole weekend, and I loved Chicago so much that I stayed.

"I'd dance at the clubs and be so good at it that some of the owners would pay me to get on the go-go boxes and do some of the moves. Someone else gave me a chance as a teacher a few years ago. He saw me dance at one of the clubs. I had new moves since disco was just becoming hot in Chicago. He hired me as a teacher at his studio." Dex rubs his hand down his face, smoothing his mustache. "Most of his clients were older, so I learned to teach the waltz, the foxtrot, and all that bullshit from him. He died a couple years later, and I started my own joint." He looks up at me and smiles. "Would you believe that after all this time, my waltz classes are where my money is? The old people still flock here. You should see Felix teach the tango."

I look around the space, nodding. It's a beautiful studio, and I'm being offered a job. Maybe Dex's background is why he's taking pity on me. He knows a broke, unemployed, and desperate person when he sees them.

Dex pushes off the wooden railing. "Let me show you your desk and the storage room."

I step down from the dance floor and let him put his hand on my back again as he leads me back to the lobby.

"Thank you for letting me come here and giving me a chance," I say in a soft voice. He dips his head to hear me because my voice is so low.

"Of course." He stops suddenly and turns to me, chewing on the inside of his cheek. "Did you think we wouldn't hire you after last night?"

I nod and look around the room to avoid meeting his eyes. I still can't come to terms with how far I let it go with perfect strangers last night. It's so out of character for me, and I've never had to think about consequences like that.

"I thought you'd be angry."

He sputters a laugh and puts his hands on his hips. My gaze follows his hands, and I find myself staring at the waistband of his faded blue jeans. "Why would you possibly think we'd be angry with you?"

"I, uh, left you guys without returning the favor."

"Who says we needed the favor returned?" Dex asks, tilting his head to the side with the sexiest smile I've ever seen.

Crap. I've never thought of men as sexy before. How much has changed in just a few days? How much more could they teach me?

"I don't know much about sex and stuff, in case that wasn't obvious."

His face softens. Damn, he's been nothing but kind to me, and I'm ruining this. I watch as he walks to the percolator and picks up a paper cup off the stack. "Cream or sugar?"

"Neither."

His body stays in place, but his head turns to look at me. A lock of hair flops over his forehead. "Dangerous choice. You are full of surprises."

He pours the coffee, and I take the cup from Dex, only to immediately slosh it on my pants as Felix comes through the door so fast that the handle hits the wall. He's holding two paper bags of cleaning supplies, and even Dex startles at the way Felix enters the room.

Felix and I stare at each other for a few moments, and his dark eyes tell me he never expected to see me again.

Green with Envy

Felix

What the fuck is she doing here? I thought Dex was kidding about giving her a job – like the guys in Hollywood make women sleep with them for jobs and then don't hire them. If I'm going to be trapped in this job with Ms. Goody-Two-Shoes every day until I can get rid of her, I'm going to stab my eyes out with a fork.

Dex just had to go and give her a job so she wouldn't be easy to get rid of. Unfortunately for her, I always get rid of them. He's mine. The world can fuck right off.

"Hi, Felix," the angelic burden practically coos when she sees me.

She can't even keep coffee in a cup, as evidenced by the mess now on the floor. I bet she can't dance to save her life. A simple look at her mousy hair that isn't so feathered and fun today, and

I know she'll be gone in two weeks flat. Obviously, someone trussed her up like the prize hog at the county fair last night. My mouth moves into what I hope looks like a genuine smile and cross the room to take her hand like a true gentleman. Dex grins at me, but I don't pay attention. This is a show for him, but I need to make it look like it's real. That I like her.

"Hi, Nicole. I forgot you were coming." I set down the bags full of bleach, scrubbing brushes, and coffee on one of the lobby chairs and turn to take her in.

I'm not impressed.

"Let me show you your work area," I say, leading her to her desk. "I hope you'll like it here. It's good to see you again."

My tongue hurts even saying it.

Dancing is my thing. Our thing. By "our thing" I mean Dex and me. Nowhere in there is this Nicole person. She may be fun to fuck, and I love to watch Dex's eyes light up when we have a new partner, but I need to get rid of her pronto. She's killing my mood and will be a complete distraction for Dex.

That's why I have to be careful with her in my space. Sneaky. Play nice. Dex is not only my lover, boss, and roommate. He's my best friend, and I know him like anyone else knows their best friend.

I can count on three things with Dex Holden: He gives great head, he loves unconditionally and hard when he does fall in love, and he tires easily of people he doesn't give a shit about.

I hope this bitch is the latter.

Did I enjoy eating a pussy the other night? Yes. It's been a long time since I've given a woman an orgasm so hard her toes curled into my shoulders. Would I fuck the hell out of her? Sure. Especially if Dex watches, holds her down, or lets me go second. Some men like to go first, but I like his seconds. They're so much...wetter.

But fall in love or even do anything but tolerate her doe-eyed bullshit?

Never.

She looks down at the desk like she's avoiding looking at me. The previous secretary left her calendar blotter on last month, so I rip the page for Nicole and wad the paper up before throwing it in the trash can. She toys with the pens in the container and throws one with a chewed cap into the garbage. I can't blame her there.

I nod around the area like I'm seeing it for the first time. "It's not much, but it's home. You can bring stuff in. A plant, maybe. You look like the kind to take care of plants. I bet you knit too."

She misses my condescending tone. "Am I the only one that works here?" she asks.

Dex circles the desk and stands next to her. I can practically see the crackling energy between them, and I narrow my eyes at the space between their arms.

Don't growl. Don't growl. Neutral expression. She can't know that you'll ruin her life and send her packing if she dares do more than let Dex be an extra hole for him to use.

"We have a co-teacher that comes in to help with waltz class. The women seem to like her better. Her name is Debra. You're the only assistant."

"OK, so this really is my desk." She sits in the office chair and twirls around in the seat before running her hands over the top. Dex practically preens next to me.

Fuck, he really thinks she's adorable. I can even admit she is...to a point. She's like a cutesy song you can't stop singing but annoys the shit out of you that it's stuck in your head.

"I'm going to put the supplies away," I say, passing Dex and running my hand over his chest. His eyes flick to me, and I see love in them. Love for me. Love for our relationship. All is not lost here.

I head to the storage room, and he clears his throat. "Nicole, I don't want you to feel awkward around us. We can all be professional. You say the word if something makes you uncomfortable."

"I understand." She looks around the desk and picks up the yellow phone. "Do I dial 9 to get out?"

"Nope. Just the standard seven digits. If you have to call long distance, let me know so I can put it in the budget. You mostly get calls, though. Unless I need something delivered, you won't call out much."

The small talk is killing me. *Get rid of this little twat, Dex.* I place the cleaning spray on the storage shelf a little harder than necessary.

"We'll need you to make a pot of coffee before each class starts," Dex directs, and Nicole looks at the percolator in the corner like it's an obstacle course contraption she'll have to scale. God, I hope one of the students complains about her shit coffee. Maybe Dex will fire her then.

I watch them as he shows her where things are, and I listen as he tells her how to use the phone, where to find the coffee, and where the dusters and cleaning supplies are, making sure to smile when Dex jerks his thumb in my direction. As soon as they look somewhere else, I roll my eyes.

I need to show authority here so that Nicole knows, in no uncertain terms, that Dex is mine. We share, of course, and we've talked about bringing someone else into the relationship for a while. Both of us eventually want children. Dex gets more successful every year, and we've been together so long now that I can't remember where I begin and he ends.

But this woman is not it.

She may be seducing Dex with her innocent doe eyes and her "I don't know how to make coffee in a percolator" bullshit, but she doesn't fool me. She'll end up in the dump heap like every other woman he brings home for us. We need someone confident. Someone not so needy.

I glance at her again and notice her slouched shoulders like she wants to hide from the world. I have her number. This is a woman who's been taught to hide from the world her entire life, and she can keep on being invisible as far as I'm concerned.

Dex looks for me over his shoulder. When our eyes meet, he smiles. I know this man loves me. He loves me with his whole heart, and I love him just as fiercely. It'll take a special woman for us both to welcome her into the life we have.

I wait until Nicole is only paying attention to Dex and has stopped fiddling with the typewriter and trying to find the correction tape. I need her to see what Dex and I have – what she'll never have.

Without hesitation, I close the space between us and pull Dex to me, our hips flush. My hardening dick rubs against his. It's handy we're around the same height because I know exactly when he's happy to see me. I nuzzle his cheek, and Nicole inhales through her nose behind me. "When you're ready for me to show you a couple new moves I learned, come find me in the studio."

I place a soft kiss on his bowed lips and hum as I pull away. Stalking to the studio doors, I open them and then look over my shoulder, only to find Dex following me, his eyes already hooded. Something tells me Nicole can't drop to her knees and give Dex a perfect afternoon blow job like I plan to do as soon as I shut the studio door.

Dex knows what he's in for as he stalks toward me. Nicole squints behind me, practically glaring, if a Suzy Sunshine can even do that. I wink at her before I close the door.

This is going to be easier than I thought.

Fondue Favors

Nicole

This is going to be harder than I thought.

I've never worked as an assistant. It's also hard when Dex, who I like very much and gives me nervous butterflies in my stomach every time he comes to my desk, obviously enjoyed time with Felix yesterday afternoon. Dex came out of the studio twenty minutes after Felix told him he wanted to show him new moves. Dex's hair was askew, and I caught him adjusting the zipper on his pants, his cheeks still flushed with what I don't think was dancing.

Did they have sex in there? Can sex happen that fast? How does it work when men have sex together? I mean, I know the basic mechanics of it, but is there some special item they need to...make things work?

I put my head in my hands, thinking about how there's so much I don't know, and I don't have anyone I can ask except for Tima. That seems like an awkward conversation.

Sheltered. I've been sheltered and coddled my entire life. Even when adults talked about what my mother called "heavy petting," I was told to cover my ears. My entire sexual education from my mother was that my husband would know what to do, and I should listen to him for guidance and make myself available to his needs whenever he asked. I was told that any penis slipped inside me could get me pregnant, and I was to avoid that at all costs until marriage. Men were seen as lecherous beings who only wanted one thing. I remember Grandma telling me that women are like a thermostat. Men always run hot, and it's our duty to cool them down to something normal.

Are men so animal-like that they can't control themselves? Is this the sexism that I hear whispers of, only in reverse? Why are women in charge of harnessing a man's control? Shouldn't he do that himself?

Since I've moved here, I've seen a different side of things. Tima doesn't seem to cool any man down. Neither does Mariam. I sure didn't cool Dex and Felix down the other night. Truth be told, the more I see Dex around the studio, the more I want to do it again.

"Hey, Nicole," Dex says cheerfully. I lift my head, trying to smile. Dex is looking at me with kind eyes and holding out a red rose. "I thought you could decorate your desk with it."

I look around for Felix. I don't know what it is, but I don't think he likes me as much as Dex does. Call me crazy.

"It's a nice day and not too cold. Want to grab some lunch?"

I eye the bottom desk drawer. "I probably shouldn't. I brought a bologna sandwich."

Dex squints. "Bologna? Baby, you can have bologna tomorrow. Today, you get fondue. Boss's treat." He holds out his hand and has my jacket held open for me before I can notice him retrieving it. I slide my arms into it, and Dex ties the belt for me. As his hands whisper over the fabric, I can't help but watch his eyes. His smile.

He enjoys taking care of people.

Desire moves up my body. At least, I think it's desire because I very much want to touch him. Feel his mouth on me. And I very much want to feel that mustache rub against my thighs again.

I grab my purse from the drawer, glance at my sandwich in its orange Tupperware container, and lament the carrot sticks in the plastic bag that are sure to go to waste.

I've never eaten fondue in a fancy restaurant, but Dex leads me to a cafe a few blocks down. He jabbers about the studio and remarks that he's happy I decided to work with him. He happily talks about a couple movies he and Felix have seen lately and asks if I like going to the movies. I'm so enraptured by the sound of his voice and his hand in my own that I almost forget to answer.

He holds my hand in a way that I've never experienced with other boys. It's practically childlike, and he even swings my hand like I used to swing my mother's when we'd go for walks.

"We've seen *Star Wars* eighteen times. I guess they're making a sequel. Can you believe it?" he asks as he opens the door to the restaurant.

"I've never seen it," I mumble. I'm not big on movies, but if Dex is going, he can see it a nineteenth time with me.

"We'll have to fix that," he says, hanging up my coat on the old-fashioned coat rack by the door.

Dex tells the hostess that we need two menus, and I follow the woman and Dex to a corner booth that's tucked away from walking traffic. The booth has leather seats and a single car-nation in a canning jar. Cloth napkins are rolled with normal utensils as well as two fondue sticks.

"Why two?" I ask Dex as soon as the woman walks away.

"One for sweet. One for savory." He leans over the table. "Have you gone out for fondue?"

I shake my head and put the sticks down, one on either side of my menu. "I had it at group parties at church, but we used toothpicks."

He shrugs. "To be fair, that's more sanitary in a big group." Hell, he's so kind and rolls with my small-town stories without any disdain or making fun of me. I like that about him.

The waitress introduces herself and puts a stack of small plates in the center of the table by the flower. She reads off a list of specials, but my mind spins. I look to Dex to take the lead.

He smiles at me, nods in understanding at my wide eyes, and thankfully orders for both of us.

"We'll have iced tea to drink, salads for both of us, and a Wisconsin cheese pot with sourdough. We'll want a melted chocolate pot with strawberries, grapes, and graham crackers for dessert."

Dex hands the menu back to the waitress, and my stomach growls at the thought. Now...what does one talk to a man about when that man is your boss, just bought you fondue, and has eaten the hell out of your pussy?

"Are you enjoying work so far?" Dex asks, clearly not feeling as awkward about being face-to-face with only the table between us.

"I like it. It's quiet, and the old people are nice. I can't believe how many elderly folks there are who take dance classes. I think half of them are here for Felix, though."

"He's very popular with the widows," he chuckles, taking a sip of the iced tea the waitress sets in front of him.

She sets a glass in front of me, and I take a pink packet of sweetener out of the container at the edge of the table. I busy myself with sweetening my tea and adjusting my utensils as Dex looks at me, his eyes focused like he can't wait to hear what I'll say next.

The silence stretches between us until I guess he can't take it anymore. "There's a contest coming up for all studios and dance teams in Chicago," he says with clear excitement in his voice. His eyes are ablaze with joy, and he reaches into his back pocket. "A bike messenger brought it over a few days ago. All the studios in town are invited to compete. Should be a good time, and it's great exposure."

He flattens a blue paper with curly, black writing I can't read upside down. "I don't desperately need the prize money, but this kind of exposure can give me that little nudge I've been needing for a year."

"What kind of nudge?" I ask.

"I want Holden Dance to be a chain. Felix deserves his own studio. He'll have one, and I'll run the other. I'll be able to hire more help. More full-time help – not part-time help of people with a few slick moves."

The waitress brings our salad, and I pour the little cup of house dressing over the greens and tomatoes, soaking the vegetables. "That's great. Who is your partner?"

Silence.

When I look up and see Dex staring at me with a smile on his face, my stomach sinks into the floor. "No, absolutely not, Dex!" I shake my head so hard that my hair comes loose from its barrette. "You've seen me dance."

"I'll teach you. How hard can it be?"

"For someone like me? Hard. Just..." My voice trails off, and I look around the restaurant like a waitress will appear and help me out of this situation. "I know you're a teacher, but I'm sure you have a student that'll be better than what I have to offer."

"You can offer a lot." He puts a hand on mine, and I almost reconsider. The warmth of his hand makes me want to accept his offer and train twenty-four hours a day to make him proud.

"Like what?" I screech. "Comedic entertainment?"

He laughs. "You are funny, Nicole." He wags his finger at me and spears a tomato from his salad. He pops it in his mouth and chews before answering. "You're perfect for it."

I nearly sputter my mouth of food. "Perfect?" I grab a drink of tea because I'm practically choking. "Perfect?"

"I knew it when I saw you at the club the other night."

"Did you hire me because you wanted me to participate in this?" I ask, leaning forward and whispering.

"Absolutely not!" He looks offended, but I can't be sure if he's serious or playing with me.

"I feel betrayed." I squeeze my eyes shut. "Oh God, is that why you guys...you know?"

"Ate your sweet little box?"

I put my face in my hands, and my elbows thump against the table so hard that the dishes rattle.

"No way!" Dex leans back, ignoring his salad and putting his arm over the leather back of the booth. "That was just a perk."

"I'm not a professional dancer. Don't you have a Doris or Maude that can dance with you? It'll be quaint and cute. Why not Felix?"

Dex raises an eyebrow and smirks. "Get real. This is Chicago in the seventies, baby, but it's still not ready for that yet."

I blow out a sigh. "Noted."

"I need a woman who will captivate the judges, and I knew it was you as soon as I saw you innocently standing by that bar. The judges will take one look at you and see what I did. I saw an innocent beauty who captured my attention immediately. I can teach you confidence and swagger. Hell, you should have met Felix before I took him under my wing."

"Felix didn't have swagger?"

"Not a drop," Dex says, waving his hands. "Bad skin, horrible hair, and said things like, 'Golly, gee whiz.'"

I laugh despite myself and move back from the table as the waitress brings a salad-bowl-sized fondue pot of steaming cheese and two plates of bread, one for each of us to reach easily. Dex uses a fondue skewer and stabs a sourdough square. I watch him while he dips it into the cheese and sets it on a small plate. Steam comes off it, and he sits back, obviously waiting for it to cool.

His eyes meet mine again. "I can teach you. You're beautiful, Nicole, whether someone has told you or not. There's something captivating about you. It's a cross between innocence and intrigue. Just for the record, I hired you because I thought you'd be a hard worker, and you have been in the little time you've worked for me."

He watches me imitate what he did with the fondue, and I tentatively test the food, letting the salty cheese coat my tongue. He watches my eyes flutter with the sheer deliciousness of it. Cheese. Glorious cheese. I think I like this kind of fondue, and I just found my favorite restaurant.

"Help me."

"Why should I?" I mean it to be playful, but it comes out challenging.

"I'll pay you extra."

I roll my neck. He knows how to twist the knife. "How much we talking?"

He taps the fondue skewer and dips another piece of bread into the cheese as he thinks. "I'll pay your salary we agreed on plus whatever your rent is for the next three months."

Holy shit. I can't turn that down.

"I still think you could find someone better."

Dex leans forward a bit more until I'm worried he'll get cheese on his shirt. "Here's the thing. I want someone I can teach. If you're partnered with someone else before me, you learn their moves – how they feel - and you'll anticipate their footwork. You're clay I can mold. You'll learn how my body works." I blush at his words, and my heart pounds so hard I think he can hear it. "I'll learn how your body works, and I'll know how to respond to it. I'll know when you hurt, and I can make it stop. I'll learn when you're in the zone, and we can be in it together."

My chest heaves with something I can't place, but I want to crawl over the bread, salad, and cheese to embrace him.

He knows he has me. I'm sure my eyes are dark pits of desire. He picks up his skewer and brings the cheese-covered bread to his mouth, dragging his tongue over it while he looks into my eyes. "Dancing with a partner you know well is like making love, Nicole. When done right, it can push us both into the stratosphere so much that you never want to be without that person."

I clear my throat and try to control my body. My panties are never going to be the same, though. "And what if I do it wrong?"

"That's why you have me. We also have three months to get you ready."

I look around the restaurant because I can't look at him. He's already shown me a world I've never seen, never dreamed of. I'm working at a dance studio, and I'm now the kind of person who's had two men go down on her in the same night.

Now he wants me to enter a dance contest? There will be judges, other dancers with years of experience, and I'll have to spend even more time with him.

Spending more time with Dex Holden is both a blessing and a curse. I'm already enamored with him so much that I'm considering entering a contest and risking tripping over my own feet.

We eat in silence, and I realize Dex is a professional at getting what he wants. He doesn't push or nag further. He changes the subject to work and how he needs me to order some cleaning items and make a few calls for him. We clean out the cheese pot, and the waitress appears with the melted chocolate pot and the fruit and graham crackers Dex requested.

Orgasmic sweetness explodes in my mouth as Dex chatters on about starting Latin dance classes because he thinks they'll be popular. He raves about disco and how it's made his career, but he thinks it's on the way out and only has a few more years before it's replaced by the next big thing. When the next big thing happens, he's going to be ready and get in on it at the ground floor. He also wants to buy the club after he gets a second studio set up. He'd keep it as a disco bar until disco moves on, and he'd do regular remodels with whatever music style is in vogue. I marvel at his business sense and his ability to pivot.

We're almost at the bottom of the chocolate pot before I bring it up again. "What if I let you down?" I ask. "I'll feel horrible if you don't get your other location. Felix will never forgive me, that's for sure. If you don't get the other location, you won't buy any club."

Dex puts his hand on mine and runs it as far up my arm as he can go with a table of food separating us. "Let me worry about Felix. Besides, we only need to place to get a decent amount of prize money and get my name out there. If we come in third, I'll be tickled pink. I got you." He grins at me and pulls out cash to pay our bill. "Is that a yes?"

"I'm thinking."

He lifts my hand and presses a kiss to the center of it. "Be wild with me, Nicole. Let's go on an adventure."

He knows just how to twist the knife with me. I have never had an adventure, and I'm desperate for one.

"I really hope I don't regret this."

Dancing Queen

Nicole

"Remember how I told you that disco is something you have to pace yourself with?" Dex asks as Felix sits cross-legged on the floor nearby.

I stand at the side of the dance floor and lean against the railing in the pink leotard I borrowed from Tima's donation clothing box. It shows a little more skin than I'm used to, but I'm afraid to do something wrong or not dress cool enough for the guys. I'm always unsure how much I can touch Dex or even look at him. Felix watches us an awful lot, and I wish I could pry his brain open to know what he's thinking.

"I think so," I say.

Felix bites his lip and studies the floor like he can't stand to look at me. Even if he's being an ass, I don't want to let him down. He's put in the work with Dex and is nothing but professional to his students. He deserves his own dance studio, especially if it will make *Dex* happy to give it to him.

"Forget that for the contest. This is different. Your movements will need to be crisp and clean since you'll have five minutes to wow the judges. Same moves, good flow without being too stiff. Bigger. Tighter. But not too tight to appear stuffy. Show the fuck off with me. Have a little attitude. Can you do that?"

"I've never had an attitude in my life."

"We're going to fix that because everyone likes to watch someone with a little edge to them. Some excitement. You'll do well with it because you have an innocence about you. If you can add a bit of sass to it, just to throw off and fascinate the judges, it'll boost our chances. It's a great combination."

Huh. I wonder if that's true for more than dance contests. Thinking about it, I get a kick out of watching Tima's train-wreck dating life, and I can't take my eyes off Dex and his forbidden relationship with Felix.

I take a deep breath. Edgy. Exciting. I can be those things. I should trust Dex will teach me.

He holds out his hand for me to join him in the center of the dance floor. "Felix, can you hit the music?"

Felix smiles at Dex but glares at me as soon as he's at the record player and Dex is facing away from him. My heart sinks because I know Felix desperately wishes he *could* enter the contest with Dex. Am I the second fiddle? It sure feels like Felix is doing everything he can to show me he outranks me here.

I take Dex's offered hand. The smell of him up close makes my knees tremble, but I have nothing to hang on to but him. Would leaning on him be weird in front of Felix?

Dex smiles at me and moves his hands up my shoulders, massaging them. There are already wet spots on his armpits because he and Felix worked on some class sequences before my training. A white sweatband is wrapped around Dex's head, and the hair around it is dark and wet.

His hands are warm as they trail down my arms until he lets go at the tips of my fingers. "You look at me," he says. "Smile for me. Do not worry about the judges. This isn't gymnastics, and you're not that Nadia gal. You don't smile for them or show them emotion. You show all attention to your partner. Meet my eyes unless I'm turning you. Then, look straight at your eye level with a smile on your face like you're above all of it. Don't look down or up. Got it?"

"I think so." I glance at Felix again, who sets his jaw. His eyes are dark, but I don't know if they're dark with desire for Dex or anger at me.

Dex waves his hand, and Felix sets the needle down on the record. The first notes of the routine music fill the silence.

"We're going to start pressed together and shimmying in place with my arms around you. Eyes on me like we're in love." His voice is soft when he says it, and he presses his forehead against mine while simultaneously tilting my chin up to his lips like we're lovers.

Felix inhales behind Dex and says something I don't catch under his breath. I don't dare take my eyes off Dex, though.

Dex's hands come to my hips, and we grind against each other. His eyes momentarily flutter like he doesn't want to let go of me, but he soon moves to the first move of our dance – a simple sidestep. It takes a few moments, but I eventually find my rhythm with it and even add in the jaunty bounce and a bit of boob shake I've seen other women do before stepping to the other side.

Dex waves his hand, and Felix stops the record. "Did I do something wrong?" I ask. "Too much boobie shake?"

"Nope," Dex says, pushing a loose tendril back as I tighten my low bun and take a deep breath. "We're just going to get one section right before we move on. We'll hold ourselves steady, forehead-to-forehead, for an eight count before we move to the side. Left first. Let me lead. Always."

"Yes, sir," I say, giving a small salute and silently wondering who leads when Dex and Felix dance together. Something tells me it's Dex.

Before I know what's happening, Dex's forehead is back on mine, but this time he kisses the tip of my nose. "Is that part of the dance?" I ask.

"No. That's just thanking you for trying this, Nicole. It means a lot to me. It also means a lot to Felix."

I look over Dex's shoulder and find Felix gripping the record player needle so hard I worry it'll snap. "Yeah, he looks super happy I'm doing this. Thankful, even."

"Give him a chance. He'll come around. He's had me to himself for years," Dex whispers. Have he and Felix discussed me? Dex said he and Felix wanted someone in their relationship. Have they discussed me as a possibility?

Why does that idea scare the shit out of me and excite me at the same time?

Dex waves his hand, and the music starts again. If Felix is so mad, why does he cater to Dex's every whim like they're an old married couple? Is that love? Tolerating your partner's bullshit because it makes them happy?

Whatever it is, I grow more fascinated with their relationship each day. I see them pass by each other and drag their hands over whatever they can reach on the other's body – hands, shoulders, and even ass when no students are around. I watch Dex smile at Felix as Felix coaches a class of fourth graders through warmups. I follow Felix's eyes as Dex teaches Foxtrot footwork to a retirement center group.

The music starts again, and I hold the eight count, forehead-to-forehead with Dex. His arms are around me, and he slouches a little while still holding a respectable dance posture that will be enough for the judges, but it allows us to be face-to-face. He's inches from me, and I yearn to lean up and kiss him.

It suddenly hits me that I haven't. Even when they went down on me the other night, I didn't kiss either one of them. Is that normal? Should we have started with kisses and discussed favorite foods and colors before I let them lick me senseless?

Dex and I start our steps left and right, and I keep up with him this time, surprising myself. We try it a third time, and I have it down pat so well that Dex teaches me the next sequence where we pull away from each other and do matching arm movements.

We work on just those moves for hours as I get them down perfectly. Once I have the movements, Dex fusses with my posture while I do the choreography without him. By the end of two hours, I'm crisp, confident, and feel like a pro when Dex and I try it one last time.

"I knew you could do it," he whispers. "We'll work on the behind-the-neck arm work as we spin tomorrow."

He pulls me in for a hug and lifts me a little. As he turns me around, I catch a glimpse of Felix by the record player, a frown lining his face.

As soon as Dex sets me down, I wave and smile at Felix. I should be kind to him. This is probably hard, and I can't deny that he's attractive.

But there's something dangerous about him. Scary. He doesn't like me, and I spend a good chunk of my days thinking of ways to change his mind. I keep the storage room clean, answer all calls professionally, and bring him paper cups of coffee when I make a fresh pot. I've tried dressing more modern, taking to raiding Tima's discarded outfits meant for the charity shops, in the hopes that Felix will like me if I dress more like the girls at the club and do my hair like them. I want him to compliment me just once.

Dex is the bright spot of my day, though, and I wake up excited in the morning, wondering what he'll bring me when he comes to work. A flower? Today it was a cookie he bought me as he passed by a bakery. He's a wonderful boss, too. He's professional, especially in front of students, but there's a look in his eyes as we pass each other or speak – like he knows what I taste like and wouldn't mind tasting me again.

It's the first time I've been desired, and I'm scared Felix will put a stop to all of it. Why can't he like me? Get to know me?

I very much want to be his friend.

Hard Truths

Dex…Two Weeks Later

Felix removes his belt a little harder than usual as he storms through the apartment. He's angry, but I can't help but think about how he does the same belt-unfastening routine before sex. Seeing it has me with half an erection. He tosses the belt across the room as I follow him into our bedroom, removing my own shirt before throwing it into the basket at the edge of our bed.

I set my jaw and stand in front of him, hands on hips. "You've been an asshole for the last couple weeks. She's working hard and getting it down. She's improved. Care to tell me why you're so mean to her? She hasn't done anything but work hard at the studio and even smile at you when you walk into a room. Fuck, Felix, she brings you coffee like she's your personal secretary and not mine."

He pulls his own shirt over his head, discards it on top of mine in the basket, and glares at me. "Why her? What the fuck is so special about Nicole?"

I sarcastically laugh and head to the adjoined bathroom. I pick up my toothbrush, not really wanting to fight with him, but he's behind me and wrapping his arms around me before I can get the paste out of the tube. "I just love you," he says. He kisses my shoulder. "I know we've talked about bringing a woman into our relationship, but I don't like *her*."

"You seemed to like her just fine a couple weeks ago when you ate her pussy like a starving man. It was quite exuberant, and I don't know if I've ever seen you enjoy the taste of pussy like that before." I stare at him in the mirror, our eyes locking. "Admit it. You find her fascinating."

"She's different."

I finally turn to face him. "That's exactly it, Felix. I like her!"

"Well, I don't! Shouldn't we both actually like the person if we're going to invite them into our relationship? It's not just you here, Dex. It's not just you who will share your life with a person. Your bed. Shouldn't I get a say?"

"Fine," I nod and turn back to the sink to resume my nightly routine. "You're right. I'm listening. What's wrong with her? Not pretty enough for you? Is it that she's from a small town and doesn't kiss your city-boy ass?"

He looks at the floor and pulls his pants off behind me. Even though we're arguing, a chill moves down my naked back. He's close enough that I feel his breath on my neck when he blows out his exasperated breaths.

He kicks his pants back into our room and adjusts his cock in his briefs before answering. "She's pretty enough when done up. Pretty plain otherwise. But that's not it. I could look past that because she's pretty in a small-town, girl-next-door way. I may not see it much around here and in our circle, but I can see how someone would think she's attractive."

"She's real, Felix." I tap my toothbrush on the sink in frustration, the tapping sound echoing through the room. "These women we've been bringing around are not. We know she can be dressed up if she wants to go out, but I like her just the way she is."

"You want reasons I don't like her, but I want reasons why you *do*!" he yells. His voice level doesn't scare me, though. I know the timbre and tremble. He's the scared one. "I see *nothing* when I look at her."

I spit my wad of toothpaste out and reach for a washcloth to wash my face. I yank it off the towel rack a little harder than necessary. "Fine. She feels like home to me. I don't know why."

"Home?" Felix laughs. "You were treated like shit at home."

I brace my hands on the counter and stare at our reflection in the mirror. "Not that home. The home I want. Safety. Security."

He presses his forehead on my back between my shoulder blades, and it fucking kills me. His hands reach around and grip my abdominals, and I can't help but cover his hands with my own. "I thought I was your safety?" he asks, his breath whispering across my back.

"You are. You always have been. But I met her, and just..." My voice trails off. "It was like when I met you. I recognized the feeling. When I met you, I felt like I could tell you everything without judgment. We were the same sexually, both bisexual with the same type of woman."

"That's obviously changed," he grumbles into my skin.

"My feelings for you haven't. Can't you give her a chance? She's not some hideous she-beast that I brought home. She's a little shy and mousy, but she's also young and from a small town. Were you any different?"

He inhales and shakes his head against my skin. I obviously hit a sore spot. Felix wasn't the sexy mother fucker he is now when I met him.

"She's working hard for us. She's kind. I like the way she looks at me and the way I'm excited to go to work to hear about anything going on in her life."

"Yes, I'm sure her stuffed bear collection is riveting."

I let go of his hands and roll my neck. I don't like the way he talks about her. I'm enamored by her. She's real to me. Not some woman that gets around and then runs out our door as soon as light creeps through the blinds. She's sweet like a bag of candy, and I don't understand how anyone could be mean to her. I can't stand not seeing her, and if I had my way, she'd be moving her suitcases in and sleeping on the other side of me in bed at night. I long to curl around her and pull her to my chest while Felix is at my back, warm and hard.

"You haven't given her a chance."

"I can't guarantee I will. Can't you accept that maybe she isn't the one we've been waiting for?"

I pull my mustache trimmer out of the drawer and flip it on. "If you'd give her a chance, she might be. Either way, I want to date her. If she isn't someone you think you can connect with, will you at least allow me to see her?"

He pulls away and stares at me. "You want to keep her separate? Like we have some open relationship or something?"

"You're not listening, and I feel like I'm talking in fucking circles, Felix. I love you. You're my person. But we both want someone else. I guess we didn't think it through that agreeing on that person would be harder than we thought."

The buzz of the clippers muffles his response, but his hands come to my shoulders, and he massages from my neck down to my ass.

I flip off the clipper and toss it on the counter with a frustrated grunt. "I guess we didn't think about if we'd both jive with the person we brought into the relationship. It never seemed like you were in a hurry."

"I'm not. That's why I think we should wait." He brushes a couple mustache hairs off the front of my chest and presses a kiss to my back. "Someone may come along that we both fall for."

"I don't know if lightning always strikes that way with one person, much less with two people involved. Can't you trust me that I'll pick someone amazing and then you give her a try to see if you can become friends with her?"

"You're asking to date her without me?"

"I want to get to know her. If I click with her romantically, I want you to give her a chance."

His eyes droop, and my heart clenches in my chest. "Will you still make time for me? For us?"

"Of course. I love you so much."

Felix meets my eyes in the mirror, and they darken as I watch. A shadow passes over his face, and his jaw hardens, but it's not in anger. I know that look.

He places one more small kiss on the nape of my neck, and then I can't see him as he disappears behind my shoulders, kissing his way down the middle of my back until he reaches my tailbone. He swirls his tongue over the spot just above the waistband of my own briefs.

Without waiting for direction, I bend over the sink as Felix ruthlessly shoves my underwear down my legs. I step out of them in compliance when they reach my ankle, and I stay bent over at the waist as Felix places one hand on my back, holding me in position.

With the other hand, he taps my inner thigh, a silent direction to widen my stance. My hand comes to my hardening dick in anticipation of what I'm going to get. I've been with Felix long enough to know that he knows exactly what to do to me to get his way.

He won't get it this time. I'll let him have his night with me, but I'll still bring her a cookie, a magazine, or even a flower tomorrow. He won't control me this way. But the key to Felix has always been to let him think he gets what he wants but let him think it's his idea when my plan works out.

My own plan is to get Felix used to Nicole, have him around her until he can't stand it anymore, and let him feel like a genius when he realizes he likes her too.

And damned if I'm not falling for her hard.

But right now, I'm going to let Felix lick my asshole while I jerk off in the sink.

His hand at my back playfully taps me, a silent command to stay. Felix and I switch the dominant role regularly, both of us wanting to be in charge. It's a compromise on many nights, and it's another reason we need a woman. A woman like Nicole, who is obviously submissive, would cater to both of our desires to be in charge. She'd fit into our relationship like apple in pie, but Felix is too stubborn to see it.

I widen even further, and Felix pulls my ass cheeks apart. The cold air hits my asshole, and I shiver as the draft feels like it moves up my spine. Felix's warm breath replaces it, and he chuckles, lightly blowing into me.

"Awfully eager tonight, Dex. Are you already hard for me?" he mumbles.

"Yes," I grunt. I want his mouth on me because I know what he's capable of.

I roll my hips into the counter under me, hoping I can accidentally hit his lips or tongue in the process. He laughs again, and I wish I could get a good angle to fist his hair and punish him for making me wait.

Slowly and agonizingly, he runs his warm tongue from my balls to my tailbone. "Is that what you want?"

"Stop punishing me."

He spits on my asshole, and it dribbles down my balls before dripping to the floor. I don't close my legs or even mind there will be a mess later.

"Do you think your little farm girl can rim you the way you like?" he taunts.

"If we teach her."

He chuckles into my ass cheeks before flicking his tongue over my puckered hole. A moan slips from my mouth. "But you're the best at it," I whisper. "Always have been."

He hums appreciatively as he circles his hands around my trunk and pulls me to him. I fist my cock and jerk it like a feral man while he licks, sucks, and flicks his tongue, rotating between my balls and my asshole. Each time he reaches my asshole, I breathe into the electric pleasure moving through my body.

I writhe against the counter, and I grimace at the bruises I'll have on my thighs from his fingers tomorrow. Pointing my dick over the sink, I wince when Felix gives my asshole one last kiss before licking up my back. I watch him reach for the lube we keep in the bathroom drawer, and I close my eyes as he grips my shoulders and inches into me.

I roll my head back and rest my face against his neck, smelling his cologne. It's such a familiar smell, and my balls tighten at what that smell so close to me means. I associate his smell with long nights in bed, his cock inside of me or him bent below me and opening himself to me.

We have sex regularly, usually with me as top, but I'm used to him playing pitcher when he has the rare urge. We know how far we can take each other, and Felix swivels his hips, waiting patiently as I adjust for him. I bite my lip at the slight pain, but it's certainly not the first time he's taken me for a ride.

After a few deep breaths, Felix pushes me over the sink again, grips my hips, and meets my eyes in the mirror. "She may get a share of your mind and heart if you choose her, but nobody can take this ass. Mine. Understand? Just like mine is yours."

I nod. "Yours."

He pulls back and then bucks into me softly, still being gentle. My hand fists my cock again as the sound of his thighs hitting my buttocks cracks through the silence. My other hand goes to the mirror, supporting us, lest I be pushed into it. The frame rattles, but it doesn't fall.

"So warm around me, Dex," Felix moans. He runs his tongue over my shoulders, nips at my skin, and then licks his way up the back of my neck.

His eyes are closed, but I wish he'd open them. Look at me. I watch him in the mirror as his mouth opens in rapture. His head lolls when it isn't leaning against me.

I jerk my cock as one of his hands moves over my torso. "That's it. Get yourself off for me. Let me hear you say my name," he coos.

I know why he wants to hear me call his name. It's not hers. I don't know how I can get him to accept Nicole with this huge chip of jealousy on his shoulder, but if he needs me to call out his name when he fucks me to prove he's still special to me, I'll do it.

My stomach tightens as his cock rubs my prostate, and Felix feels it too. He moans and utters a string of cuss words as his thighs tighten against my buttocks. When my balls contract, he pulls out and thumps his dick against me twice before releasing a warm fountain of cum on my lower back. The sound of it dripping onto the floor and the sound of his whining pleasure pushes me over the edge, and I unload into the sink, my cock twitching in my hand as my eyes flutter closed.

I call his name like he asked. It's the only name I've called out in bed for years, so it flows off my tongue without thought. A reflex.

When I'm spent, Felix pulls me to his chest and kisses my neck one last time. "I love you. See her if you must, but nothing will change us. I won't allow it."

"She's meant to fit into our lives, not come between us."

"We'll see," Felix says before playfully smacking my ass and stepping into our shower.

Come to Felix

Felix

S he's in the studio when I walk into work. The doors are wide open, and the disco ball spins above her head, flashing pink and purple lights onto the walls and floor. I place my duffle bag down on a plastic chair in the lobby and quietly walk toward the studio.

Nicole doesn't initially see me. The music is on, and she counts aloud. "One, two, three, four, turn and –

She stops suddenly when she sees my hands bracing the doorway. "I didn't mean to scare you," I say.

She silently walks to the record player and doesn't speak until she lifts the needle. "I came in early to practice. I don't want to let him down."

My heart squeezes that she's doing this for Dex. Is that supposed to manipulate me or make me like her? I can't tell because something about her is too good to be true. Nobody can be this nice, giving, and this considerate of others. She has to have an agenda.

I walk closer and turn on the main lights so the disco ball isn't the only source of luminance in the room. We both squint, but it will make talking to her easier. With the ball and the music, I find myself wanting to dance with her and get lost in the music.

"Maybe we should chat about this thing you have with Dex," I say, my hands on my hips.

She sighs and looks down at the record on the turntable, removing stray lint that really isn't there. "Maybe we should. It'd be nice to hear how you feel."

"What do you mean?"

"I like Dex. He says that you and him..." Her voice trails off, and she makes a waving motion with her hand. Her eyes squeeze shut like she can't imagine Dex and I together. "He's told me you're together, but he says things to me, and I don't understand them."

"Like what?" I ask. Please let it be something I can use to get rid of her.

"He says he wants to see me, too. Do you know about this? I just want to make sure everyone is being told everything before I go out with him."

I mentally run through ways I can use this to my advantage, but nothing comes to mind. If I tell her Dex is full of shit and just using her for the contest and a receptionist position, it could get back to him. He'll be pissed, and I could lose him. I go with the truth. "We're together, and we've been looking for someone, male or female, for a while now. Hell, Dex would have a whole commune of people he loves if he could."

Nicole flushes and bites her lip. "So, he *does* want to date me."

"It would appear so. Personally, I don't know why. I've said as much to him."

Her head lifts, and her eyes meet mine. I clock the sadness in them, and her lip trembles for a moment before she bites it, stilling herself. Huh. Surprising. I thought she'd look at her feet for the rest of the conversation.

"You don't want me here?" she asks.

I give a short nod and leave it at that. I want her gone, but I'm not in a bad enough mood right this second to tell her everything that's wrong with her. She'd never recover from being told she's too small-town for Dex. Too innocent. Too young. Maybe I'll save that for a day when it will have more bite.

"I'm so confused by all of this."

"Do you like him?" I ask. She blinks like she has to think about it. "I asked you a question, *Nicole*." I drag out the word. "Do you, or do you not like my partner?"

"Yes. I do."

"Do you want to see him romantically?"

She cracks her knuckles, and the hair on my neck raises in protest. If Dex has her stick around, that habit needs to be the first to go.

"Yes." She says it so quietly that I have to lean forward to hear it.

I walk to her until I'm about three feet away. My proximity bothers her, and I use it to my advantage. I need to assert dominance here. She may be able to play the role of Dex's new fun toy, but she'll be gone as soon as he grows bored.

Maybe that's my best plan. I look her up and down. The simple, stretchy leotard she wears is pink, and it reminds me of doll clothing. Her hair is in a simple bun at her neck, and no jewelry is on her anywhere. I study her ears. Are they even pierced? It figures she would wear clip-ons like my grandmother.

I make the decision just then. I'll do anything Dex wants me to do, short of actually going on a date with this woman. He'll be bored and get rid of her quick enough. I just have to ride it out. I'll let him have his fun. Hell, maybe I'll join in and play the dutiful boyfriend. That may actually work. The more I'm blasé toward her and the more she's just her boring self, the more annoyed he'll get.

"Dex and I made an agreement. He'd like to date you. I'll allow it."

Her nose crinkles, and it's so fucking cute I almost run my index finger down it in one swipe. As I look at her face, I notice, for the first time, a smattering of light freckles. I'm sure Dex finds them endearing, and I start to smile at the sight of them until I stop myself.

"You won't be coming with us?" she asks, jolting me out of my thoughts that she looks adorable when she's confused. Damn it.

"We don't have to do everything together. You're free to spend time with Dex as long as you understand he comes home to me at night." I look her up and down and smirk when she practically curls in on herself to avoid my disdain. "And all that...entails."

She looks at the floor and shuffles her feet. "He asked me to dinner and a movie tonight. I'd like to go. I don't have many friends here."

"Why's that?" I ask, cocking my head and clucking my tongue. "Not so many in Chicago that think small towns are cute? I bet you had a bunny or something when you were little. You just seem that type."

"Where are you from?" she asks like she's suddenly challenging me.

"Detroit."

"In Detroit or around Detroit?"

Wow, this bitch is really pushing my buttons. That's new. I grew up in the boring suburbs that popped up after the war and moved to the city as soon as the clock struck midnight on my eighteenth birthday. I couldn't get out fast enough. Not that I'd ever admit any of that to Nicole. She needs to think I was born right in the city center.

She finally looks up but still doesn't meet my eyes. She stares at my chin like she's trying to burrow into the cleft there. "I'd like to be friends with you, too. You're important to Dex."

I cross my arms. "Do you really think you fit in with Dex? Or, are you just trying him on like a pair of new shoes you'll toss as soon as they scuff? Because that's not going to fly here, Nicole. If you hurt him, you'll hear from me."

She nods, and her eyes don't move from my chin. Part of me wants to squeeze her cheeks and force her to look at me. I don't dare touch her when Dex isn't around. To do so, to touch her without it being for Dex's approval or pleasure, seems wrong. No. She's something used only for pleasure from now on. Mine or Dex's.

Nicole bites her lip like she wants to say something. I watch her struggle with speech, and part of me wants to laugh. Taunt her.

Just when I think she won't dare speak to me, her mouth opens. She licks her lips and finally looks at me without looking away. "I think I would fit in just fine if you'd give me a chance."

"Just out of curiosity, why do you want that, Nicole?" I lean my hand on the nearby record table like I'm settling in for a long conversation and interested in what she has to say. "You're not the type. What interests you about being a third in our relationship."

"Dex said it would be equal. Like a triangle."

"That's what we both want, Nicole. A third person for us to love and share our life with. Someone who would be willing to be an equal partner in everything. The business. Our family. We want that. Dex craves it like water. I've always known that. It's just the way he's built. That guy has so much love in him to give to others, it's like a snake coiled inside of him, ready to strike anyone who passes by. His family was shit. He took all the love he wasn't allowed to show them for fear of punishment and bottled it up. But he's successful now, and he's ready to pop the cork and let it flow. Hell, part of me is the same." I look away from her and idly flip through a few of the records Dex left out, just for something to do with my hands. "I have love to give. But I'm picky as fuck about who I give it to."

"Come out with us tonight."

I smirk in surprise. Her brazenness shocks me. She's never argued for or against something in the little time I've known her. "Why?"

"Dex would like it. I'd like it. I want to get to know you. I want to learn to like you, even if you're rude to me now. You just don't know me. I want to be civil to you for Dex's sake. I've never met anyone like him. I want to try something. Something new and exciting. I want to go on a life adventure."

"So, it *is* entertainment for you? This is a fun hat to try on, huh?"

Her eyes widen, and she shakes her head until the hair around her face slaps her skin. "No! I –

She's interrupted by Dex as he barrels through the door to the studio with a huge smile on his face. He's holding his black, leather briefcase full of schedules and important monthly con-tracts for students to sign.

He walks to Nicole and me like we're not having a tense conversation but simply talking about the weather. He kisses my cheek first before kissing Nicole's. Putting aside our differences for a second, Nicole and I both smile at Dex like he's the sun in our solar systems.

I guess he kind of is.

Eventually, he looks between us like he just noticed the possibility that we may have been talking without him. "How are my two favorite employees today?"

That hurt. I used to be his only favorite.

Focus, Felix. Play nice. If you can convince him you're open to this and nice, he'll get bored on his own. She'll be on the first bus back to Dogpatch. If I push and complain much more, they'll form an alliance, and it could hurt my relationship with him.

"Nicole and I were just discussing that you're taking her on a date this evening. I was offering suggestions about where you should go."

Dex smiles like I just suggested an orgy. "Is that right? Where did you suggest?"

I smile at Nicole, working to make it as much like a genuine smile as I can. "Nicole here said she's never tried escargot and really wants to try it. You should take her out for some. Top of the line." I look back at Nicole just as her face starts to turn green. "I'd also suggest a sea urchin appetizer. Maybe some blood pudding. She's never had that, either. You could really show her all kinds of cuisine tonight, Dex."

"That's amazing," Dex says, oblivious to Nicole's horror as he kisses us both on the cheek again and walks to his office, swinging his briefcase like he's out for a jaunty stroll.

"Thanks for that," Nicole whispers.

"Make sure he brings me a doggy bag," I say, turning on my heels with a chuckle.

Date Night

Dex

Judging by Nicole's face as she picks up an escargot, Felix was fucking with her. I watch and hope she'll enjoy it when she takes a bite. They're soaked in butter, so they're probably not half bad.

On a whim, I stop cutting my own steak and lean over to spear one of the snails I ordered for her, thankful they're already out of the shell. That's the hard part. I pop it into my mouth as Nicole stares, and I let the butter coat my tongue. The sensory experience of escargot is not for the weak, but the taste is orgasmic.

I close my eyes and smile as I swallow, hoping it encourages her to taste her food. It works, and she cringes before popping the escargot into her mouth.

Watching her reaction is amusing. She goes from slowly chewing with her face squished to relaxing her jaw, widening her eyes, and nodding as she greedily chews. "It's not terrible."

"I'll tell Felix you like it," I say.

"He won't believe you."

I set my fork and knife down. "I know he's hard to take, but he will come around. I have full faith in that. I've known him a long time. Trust me."

"Any tips on how I can win him over?"

"Can I ask if you're sure you *want* to win him over?"

"I do. I don't know why I'm interested in this arrangement, but I am. It's so odd. It's never been on my radar, but now that I know you and work for you, I don't want to give that up. I enjoy spending time with you, and you've both made it clear that you're a package deal. Are you sure Felix is interested in dating a third person?"

"Yes. He's always been on board. I talked to him the other night. After that talk, part of me wonders if he's always thought he'd be the one to pick the third. Neither of us thought it would be this hard to agree, but I met you and just...well, I just knew I at least wanted to get to know you. That's what this is," I say, waving between us and then around at the restaurant.

"How do I get him to like me?"

I shake my head, sigh, and pick up my utensils again. "Not a clue. Felix and I were easy when we met. We met, he came home with me, and neither one of us ever wanted him to leave again."

Nicole swallows another snail and then takes a drink of her wine. I smile at the idea of her going from a bologna sandwich kind of girl to fondue, escargot, and wine in just a few weeks. I like showing her things. I like being a new experience for her. It's fun watching her reaction to experiences, and she's under my skin already. When I'm with Felix, I wish she was with us so I could show her what we're doing. When I'm with her, I miss Felix at my side. It's horrible spending time with them separately, and I want them to get along so bad it's all I can think about.

"You're improving your dance skills. I brag about you all the time to Felix."

"He's not impressed, is he?"

I smile and go back to cutting my steak. "He's more of a visual person. He'll have to see it to understand." I meet her eyes across the table. "Come to the club with us sometime. It may help. It's also where our relationship will be welcome outside of our home. We can be ourselves. Dance together."

"Would that make Felix happy?" she asks, tilting her head.

I lean forward and cup her cheek. "It would make me happy. I know we're out on a date without him, but I want to try getting together as a group every now and then. It won't work otherwise."

The waiter brings the dessert menu as Nicole and I finish eating, chatting easily about work and the dance contest. When we pass on dessert because Nicole is too full, I pay the bill in cash and offer Nicole my arm to get up from the table.

"What next?" she asks.

I lean over to kiss her cheek. "I promised you something."

***

The theater is almost empty since the movie has been out for a year. Nicole and I take a seat in the back, and I press my hand to her thigh as soon as we settle in our seats. Talk about growth. A month ago, she would have trembled at my touch. Now, she expects it. My hand belongs there.

"I thought you said you've seen this a ton," she says. "Are you sure you want to see it again?"

"And you said you hadn't seen it at all." I turn to face her, shifting the popcorn tub to the side to look at her. "Do you want to leave?"

"No!" she practically yells. A couple a few rows in front of us glares at us, and I wave. Nicole pushes my arm down with a laugh. "I just don't want you to be bored."

The beginning starts to loud music, and I lean over until I'm right in front of her face. I shift the popcorn to the seat next to me and forget about it as I press my lips to her mouth. My cock hardens at the proximity and the way her hands slide down my chest as she opens her mouth, allowing my tongue to taste and explore. For someone who hasn't been kissed a lot, she's pretty decent at it.

And I love to taste and explore her. I love that she's so different from Felix's hardness and scruff. He takes. She gives. Both let me lead, but it's different in the execution.

I pull away from her so she can see the beginning summary. "Please let me say this just once because I think it's been on your mind. You do not bore me. OK?"

"But Felix –

I put my finger over her lips, still wet with my spit. "You're not Felix. Felix isn't you. I like both of you just the way you are. I don't need a clone of Felix because I, well, I already have Felix," I say, scratching the back of my neck awkwardly. "I really like you, Nicole. If you can get over the weirdness of the relationship dynamic, I want to continue getting to know you."

"What does that mean?" she whispers. The couple in front of us turns around to glare again, and Nicole ducks her head a bit, still looking to me for an answer.

"It means that I don't want to see other women."

She nods, and I settle back in my seat, placing the popcorn bucket between us. I take a drink from my soda and get into the movie until she wraps her arm around mine and tucks her face into my neck. "It's so damn weird, but it feels so right," she whispers. "I can't explain it. The only thing wrong is Felix hating me."

I smile against her cheek in response and watch the movie without interruption. When it's over, we hail a cab as soon as we leave the theater, and I walk her to her front door.

I look up at her building, hoping for an invitation inside for coffee...or other things. Nicole seems to be having an internal discussion about inviting me in because she opens the building door, closes it and walks back to me, opens it again, and then comes back to stand in front of me. I laugh at her indecisiveness, and her mouth opens and closes like a fish as I step forward.

I chuckle and run my hand down her nose. "It's OK. I don't want to come in if you feel like you owe me something for the night."

"I'm sorry," she says, shaking her head. "I grew up in a very different world, and I need help being different."

I grip her shoulders and gently pull her to me so I can kiss her forehead. "When you're ready, Nicole. For all of it. This is new territory for me, and it's definitely new for you. Don't worry about Felix. He'll come around. OK?"

She nods in silence, and I make the decision for her. "I like you, Nicole. I'm not going anywhere." I kiss her on her cheek one last time, not wanting to be away from her warm skin. My cock twitches to attention in my jeans as my balls disagree with me not going up to her apartment and turning her into a sex-hungry minx. But Felix is at home waiting for me. My balls won't hurt for long. "Good night."

I hold on to her hand until we're far apart and only our fingers touch. She giggles before we finally part, and I raise my hand to hail another cab.

"Good night, Dex. See you at work tomorrow."

I look back and point. "You have training tomorrow before work. Be there or be square."

Piercing Nicole

Nicole...A Month Later

"You don't have to do this," Dex says, bending down and studying my earlobes.

I take a deep breath and let it out. "I do."

"This is not a requirement for the contest, nor to date us."

Felix whispers something I can't hear out the side of his mouth. He's holding the needle, and I can tell he's downright giddy to use it. Even if I asked him to do the honors, I can tell he's happy to cause me a little pain, even if it's for a moment. Maybe that's why I asked him to pierce my ears. On some level, that he'll enjoy it. I'm also hoping it bonds us a bit as he drives the needle through my skin and hits the potato Dex holds behind my earlobe as a needle stop. I know, in the depths of my soul, that Felix isn't evil.

I hold up the simple gold stud earrings I brought over. "I need to wear posts first, so I'm sorry I can't wear the hoops I know some of the girls at the club wear. I'll still have the posts at contest time."

Dex's face falls. He'd told me that the judges will only care that I look bathed and that my dancing is on point. They won't care if I wear hoops or posts, sequins or velvet.

I want to look good for *him*.

Felix taps his foot impatiently, and I take another breath. "Do it," I say, squeezing my eyes shut and gripping Dex's hand that isn't holding a root vegetable to the back of my ear.

Felix removes the ice cube he's been holding to numb the ear lobe and pushes the needle through my skin. A whimper comes from my mouth as a pinching pain hits my ear. It's not terrible, but it reminds me of when the doctor stuck my finger for a blood test.

Removing the needle, Felix hurriedly cleans the area with alcohol, both front and back, and then pushes one of the earrings through for me, only having to swivel it a bit to find the exit hole. "All done that ear."

He quickly cleans the needle with alcohol again and we all switch to the other side. I grip Dex's hand, but I don't look away when Felix pushes the needle through my skin this time. I watch him meticulously as he concentrates to make sure the holes are equal.

If he really hated me, would he care?

Either way, I'll take him caring for me for the briefest of seconds and making sure I don't look ridiculous with lopsided earrings.

When it's done, he cleans both my ears again and steps back to make sure they look equal. My ears are hot and already swelling, and Felix examines his handy work as I look at him.

It's a rare occurrence to be this close to him and have his face an inch from mine. Up close, I notice a gold halo ringing his eyes and stubble I want to reach out and touch. Would he let me cup his cheek in the bathroom? Could I drag my finger down the cleft in his chin that I very much like?

Why do I even care? Sure, Dex loves him, and I'm definitely falling for Dex. I see Dex at work and during training, and we go out a couple times a week. But what is it about Felix that makes me want to win him over?

"All done. You can take the alcohol home if you don't have any," he says. "Oh, and you'll have to turn them a few times a day so the skin doesn't grow around it."

"Thank you, Felix. I'm sure that was fun for you."

He smiles at me, but it's a genuine smile...for once. "You didn't flinch. I really thought you'd flinch."

***

"Wine?" Felix asks as he pours a glass of white for Dex.

Dex knocks the drink back in one go, and Felix smiles. "Pace yourself, boyfriend."

"It's just been a long day," Dex says. He looks over at me as Felix hands me the bottle. "Do you like this type of wine, Nicole? We can get you something else."

"It's great. All wine tastes the same to me. One of these days, you'll have to teach me about it."

Felix sits next to me on the couch and pulls my feet into his lap, surprising me so much I startle and almost slosh wine down the front of my shirt. Neither man notices because they chat about work while Felix idly rubs my feet.

Why? I don't understand this man. One minute he looks at me like he'd drop me off at the nearest dumpster, the next he's pouring me wine and rubbing my feet. Is it a show for Dex? Or does he slip into the nice person he is when his mind is otherwise engaged away from hating me?

Dex yawns, and Felix gets up. He takes my empty wine glass and also takes Dex's. "Let's go to bed," Felix whispers, running his finger over Dex's cheek.

I'm not jealous. How am I not green with envy when I watch the man I'm starting to have romantic feelings for getting touched by another man? I would have been throwing up with fear of losing any man if I had seen that in my hometown, and I've never met a man I've liked more than Dex Holden.

I tilt my head, watching the boys interact with whispered words and loving caresses, and my heart contracts in a way I don't understand. Felix leans over and kisses Dex on the forehead before saying something I can't hear. A sudden yearning to be sandwiched between them hits me, and I stand, shaking out my legs because I don't know what else to do with my body and these feelings.

I clear my throat. "Thanks for piercing my ears, Felix, and thanks for the wine. I'll just, um, go..." My voice trails off, and I point to the door.

Dex leans forward and drops his chin. "Stay the night," he says in a husky voice.

The clock ticks in the corner of the room, and silence crackles through the air. I look at Felix, searching for a sign I should go – that he doesn't want me here – but he licks his lips as his eyes move the length of my body.

Dex stands and crosses the room until he's in front of me. When he lowers his mouth to mine, I look at Felix over Dex's shoulder. What if Felix kicks me out?

He doesn't, and I wrap my arms around Dex's neck. I tremble with nerves when I realize what Dex is asking. He's asking me to stay the night.

In his bed.

With both of them.

Does Dex want sex? I don't know the expectation, and the newness of it and the fear of the unknown set off alarms in my head. Who loses their virginity like this?

"I'm a v-virgin," I stammer. I don't know why it's the only thing I say, but it's what comes out in the moment. Both men know this, and I've told them before, but nerves take control of my body.

Felix smiles behind Dex, but it's not mean. It's kind. God, he's hot and cold.

"I know," Dex says, wiping a lock of hair back from my face. "Would you like me to be your first, or do you want to wait? Because I'd very much like to be your first."

Felix coughs behind him. "If you'd like to do it alone, I'll stay out on the couch for a bit, but I put my foot down at sleeping out here. I understand if you want your first time to be private, though."

I want to punch Felix in the dick about half the time, but some moments he makes me want to kiss him. This is one of the latter. At least he's considerate, but I can't take him away from Dex. How would he feel if I sent him to the couch? He'd seethe in anger, and I'd take the brunt of it.

And I *want* to let him watch. Something animal-like in me awakens, stretches, and roars. The sheer filth of it is a delicious concept as it bops around in my mind.

I walk around Dex and face Felix, my legs like a gelatin mold, but I'm trying so hard to be brave and discuss this like how I think an experienced adult would. "Will you hate me if I say yes?"

"No, Nicole," he says, looking at me like I'm lunch. "And I know you want him to be your first. I'll respect that."

Memories of being consumed by Felix's mouth run through my mind, and I back into Dex, probably looking for comfort since Dex is my comfort while Felix is my challenge, the villain in my love story with Dex. He's also gorgeous and unhinged, a deadly combination for a man.

"Are you scared of me, Nicole?" Felix asks. "Because I'd never hurt you."

Dex's arms wrap around my body, and he buries his head in my neck. The heat of him sears my back, even through my thin shirt, and my eyes fight to stay open.

"Unless you want me to, that is," Felix adds with a smirk.

Dex runs his hands through my hair and nuzzles my jaw. My heart pounds at the proximity of him. I could just melt back into him and let him consume me. But would Felix allow it? Why do I have such intense feelings for Dex after knowing him for such a short time? Is this love? Lust? A normal twenty-something woman with needs like Tima always talks about?

Felix drags his finger down my cheek and looks me up and down, his eyes settling on my breasts.

Tentatively, Dex cups one of my tits through my shirt. "I want you to stay," Dex whispers next to my ear. "We'll be good to you. Both of us, if you decide to go down that road. Or it can just be me. You're in charge tonight." His eyebrows raise against my cheeks as if he's telling Felix to comply.

Felix grins and cups Dex's cheek. "Of course, we'll be nice," he says. I hear the desire in his voice as it shakes, but I don't think it's for me. Dex may want me, but Felix wants Dex and is willing to play with me. I'm naïve, and even I can see that.

I must give a sign – a caress or a whimper – and I'm suddenly lifted into Dex's arms. He turns me and kisses me as he walks me to a bedroom down the hall. My eyes are closed, but I feel Felix following us. I can't hear his footfalls on the soft shag carpet, but I can feel his eyes on me as Dex crushes his mouth against mine.

Dex carries me to their bed, and I momentarily prop myself on my elbows to look around the darkened room. The bed is massive, possibly bigger than a king or two queens put together and is covered in a brocade blanket. I run my hands over the material, comforting myself with the feel of the rough fabric. Masculine fabric. There's an attached bathroom with two sinks, and I wonder which sink they'd make me use if I ever moved in with them. Dex's, I'm sure. Felix seems like a *selfish about his sink* kind of guy.

Both men get on their knees at the end of the bed. In movies and books, I've heard about how men attack the woman with desire, but both men stay at the edge of the bed in perfect patience, obviously waiting for me to give some kind of permission. Do I blink? Grunt? Demand they strip for me?

"Strip for me," I say, inhaling a horrified gasp as soon as the words are out.

Felix laughs, and it's such a comforting sound. Like we're playing together. Dex's face is still serious, and he looks at me like I'm lunch, but Felix laughs at the outlandishness of my direction.

I like making laugh in fun – not in ridicule.

Without a word, both men take their shirts off, pulling them slowly over their heads. I notice Felix's perfectly defined abdominals and his broad chest, but Dex is also admirable. His perfect, masculine body is going to be the first one I know intimately. My legs tremble at the thought of feeling that chest hair against my own breasts. My eyes flick to the outline of his hardening cock, and I watch with curiosity and excitement as he unzips his pants.

Felix also unzips his pants, albeit quicker than Dex, and I register Felix in his briefs and settling on the bed next to me, his body propped on an elbow as he watches Dex.

I've never seen a cock in real life before, and I bite my lip to keep from laughing that my first experience is like this – with two men in the room.

Dex slides his briefs down while watching my face in anticipation. He knows this is all new to me, and he studies me, waiting for any clue he's pushing me too far.

My eyes flick to his length, and I sit up to get a better look, even tilting my head. Thankfully, they don't laugh or toy with my emotions. If Felix has something to say, he doesn't open his mouth. They momentarily let me study Dex's cock as I run my eyes over the length and lean to look at the balls under it. I focus on the head and the wetness there, and I marvel that men get wet too.

Leaning forward, I press a kiss to Dex's stomach as he runs his hand through my hair and tilts his head back with a sigh. His stomach is all I can manage, though. I don't think I'm ready to take him into my mouth like Tima's told me about.

I kiss my way up from his stomach and let his chest hair tickle my nose as I work up to his neck. "Hmmm, Nicole," he whispers. "We have to get your clothes off."

They've seen me before when they ate my pussy, but my stomach still drops at the idea of getting naked for the express purpose of sex.

"Can Felix undress you for me while I watch?"

I nod, and Felix's hands are immediately at the hem of my shirt. I watch him as he lifts it off me and drops it to the side of the bed. He doesn't fling it away or ball it up. I can't pin down why he's so mean to me at work and so kind to me, even to my clothing, here in bed with Dex. Is Dex right in the fact that Felix is really nice and just needs to come around?

He unhooks my bra, and cool air hits my nipples. I resist the urge to cover my breasts and choose to lie back and allow Felix to undo my pants. He works them down my legs and then moves to the side again, letting Dex see my nakedness.

Dex must like what he sees because a growl escapes his throat as he moves on top of me. His shoulders heave with his desire, and his cock touches my thigh.

"I'll be gentle, Nicole," he says. He kisses my cheek and then places a soft kiss on my lips. "But it will still hurt for a minute."

"Like when Felix pierced my ears?"

Dex tilts his head to the side and caresses my temples with his fingers as he thinks about my question. "Yeah, I guess a little like that." He presses another soft kiss to my lips. "I'm going to make sure you're ready, though. If not, I'll get you ready."

"What do you mean re –

My words are interrupted by Dex slipping his finger between us and swiping up my center. He chuckles a little and bends down to kiss my chest. "You are definitely wet for me," he says, kissing his way back up.

I wrap my arms around his shoulders and place a kiss on his hot skin. I'm frozen in fear, but I need to do something to him so he doesn't think I'm a cold lay who won't touch him.

"Open a little more for me," he says, nestling between my thighs. The tip of his cock meets my slit, and I squeeze his shoulders in reflex. "Shhh. I'll make it feel so fucking good, Nicole. I want this to be special for you."

My eyes find Felix in the darkness. His hands are in his briefs, and he's rubbing his cock as he watches Dex and me. "Oh, I think I can always say my first time is special."

Dex smiles against my skin and pushes inside of me by about a millimeter. I still tense and arch my back as he strokes my hair. "We'll go slow."

I nod, squeezing my eyes shut.

He pushes in more.

OK, this isn't so baaaa –

Hot pain slices through me as I suddenly feel like my core is being torn up the center, but I can't move. I now know what people mean when they describe a burning pain. It burns more than pinches.

I can't breathe. Dex boxes me in, shushing in my ear. My thighs fall to the side as my body gives up the fight, not fearing anything else Dex can do to me if this is the worst of it. My subconscious gives up any fear of what damage Dex can do because it's done.

Felix watches in anticipation, of what I'm not sure. He stares at the place where Dex and I are now connected. Is he waiting his turn? Is he angry and changing his mind about this?

I get my answer after Dex swivels his hips once. I close my legs around his back, but he quickly pulls out of me. "Did I do something wrong?"

"No, Nicole. I'm just going to give you a second." I then watch in confusion as he turns to Felix with a smirk and gestures at me with his chin. "Clean her off me."

Felix licks his bowed lips and smiles before bending down and swiping his tongue up Dex's cock. Licking his lips once again, he dips to my pussy and swipes his tongue over the area from my pussy to my clit and then around my pelvic region, cleaning off whatever needs cleaning. Blood? My want? Whatever it is, my body goes limp as Dex holds my thighs apart and lifts me higher for Felix to get every inch of my skin clean.

Felix hums in approval and lifts his face a little, showing a smudge of pink on his chin. I'm frozen in shock as to what's happening, but Felix's warm tongue on my slit is as exquisite this time as it was the last time his head was between my legs. He kisses my clit and looks up at me with hooded eyes. "I'll be back if you decide you want that, but you'll need to tell him."

His mouth leaves me, and I whimper, wanting him back on my skin. I may have feelings for Dex that are something I can't identify, but Felix's mouth and body are something I've never dreamed of feeling. My eyes flick between the men, unsure which one I want more. Dex for his kindness and personality that's the closest to love for a man that I've ever felt. Felix because he excites me. Scares me.

Before I can think about it too much, Felix wraps his lips around Dex's dick and takes long pulls, bobbing his head in a rhythm as Dex fists his partner's hair. "Yeah...suck it all off me before I fuck her again," Dex whispers.

I stay still, my eyes wide as I watch something I've never contemplated, and wait for Dex to come back to me. On some level, I'm thankful for the break. I'm sore already, and my pussy throbs with want from Felix's ministrations. I'm speechless, frozen, and helpless to do anything but watch Felix suck Dex's dick. I'm surprised how much I love the look on Dex's face. I don't care that it's not me bringing him this pleasure. If anything, I'm glad Felix is here to do this – to ensure Dex will enjoy himself when I have no idea how to please any man.

Felix comes off Dex with a smacking sound and licks his lips one last time before trailing kisses up Dex's chest. When Felix reaches Dex's mouth, they kiss passionately just as Dex's finger moves to my clit. I arch into it, and my gasp breaks their kiss.

Dex silently squares between my legs again and pushes into my waiting pussy. He leans on top of me, covering my body with his own, and I instinctually wrap my legs around him. "Does that feel OK, Nicole? A bit more used to me now?"

Felix moves away, but I close my eyes. I don't know where he is, and I don't really care. I can only concentrate on the feel of Dex inside of me. A man...inside of me. The reality of what I'm doing hits, and I gasp as if shocked with myself.

"Did I hurt you?" he asks, cupping my cheek.

"No. I'm just overwhelmed."

"I can play with Felix for a bit if you want to take a break and watch." He smiles and then drops a kiss on the side of my mouth as he still thrusts into me. His eyes flutter as I think about what he said. "That's one of the benefits of the group dynamic."

Hands stroke my hair, and that's when I realize Felix is kneeling by the headboard and waiting his turn.

"I'm fine. It's just all...new. I want this, Dex."

He nods and pushes into me as I buck back in a rhythm that feels natural to me. I close my eyes and think hard about what my body is telling me to do. When I have the urge to reach down and see what Dex's butt feels like, I cup his cheeks, pulling him into me further. When I have the urge to moan, one escapes my throat, and I'm surprised when Dex responds with his own grunt.

Felix moves closer, and I finally look up at him. His erection is near my face, and I tilt my head as I examine his balls. They're the first I've ever seen up close like this. Do I do something to them? Lick them?

I don't have time to think about it too much because Dex moves my hand to my clit and swirls it around like he did the night we met. "Touch yourself. I want to feel you come around me, and Felix wants to watch. Don't you, Felix?"

"Yes," Felix whispers above me.

I do as I'm told, shutting my eyes again. I may be bold and trying new things, but touching myself in front of two men will take some getting used to.

The combined feel of Dex inside of me and my fingers on my clit sends fire up my spine. The bed rocks with Dex's thrusts, and someone holds my other hand down on the bed. I'm not certain which man it is.

"Good girl, taking him like that for your first time," Felix coos above me as he strokes my hair.

His words push me over the edge, and I bite my lip as my body trembles so hard that Dex holds me to the mattress. Felix laughs somewhere above my head, but it's not taunting. It's the sound of a man liking what he sees. I must be a sight, too. I shake so hard that my hair flops into my face, and my tits jiggle. Dex appreciates the show and bends his head just enough to capture one of my nipples, sucking on it as my orgasm rockets through me. The feel of him inside of me, his wet spit on my nipple, and my hand at my clit undoes me, and I scream Dex's name into the void as I buck like a mad woman. Stars dance over my closed eyelids.

My exuberance must excite Dex because he pounds into me hard, cursing and moaning as Felix fists my hair. "Ahh, Nicole. Fuck, baby. You feel so fucking good."

Before I realize what's happening or can react to his comment, Dex leans forward and takes Felix's cock into his mouth. He moans around Felix's dick as I buck against Dex. My eyes are level with Dex's mouth as he licks Felix, even taking one ball into his entire mouth before coming off it and leaving a trail of spit behind that drags across my cheek.

My mind whirls with the minutiae of how the position works and why it's so enjoyable for Felix, who throws his head back and closes his eyes in rapture as Dex takes another long pull on Felix's length. Dex hums a little and sends a visible shudder through Felix. Felix whines in protest as Dex pulls off his cock and kisses the tip.

"When was your last period, Nicole?" Dex asks, his voice urgent.

I shake my head a little. "Wh-what? Why are you asking?"

Dex whines, frustrated I'm making him speak. "I'm going to come so fucking hard in about thirty seconds, and I need to know where I can put it. I'm assuming you're not on the pill."

My mind spins. I didn't know there was going to be a test, and I'm in a strange situation as Felix jerks his cock near my face, angling for Dex's mouth again. Talk about pressure.

I squeeze my eyes. "Uh, three weeks ago, I think."

"You know about the rhythm method?"

I nod. It's what women in my family were taught to use when they didn't want to get pregnant. It works until it doesn't, but I've always been regular. Most women who get pregnant by watching their fertile cycles aren't regular and have no idea when they ovulate.

"Yes," I whisper as Dex takes Felix's entire cock into his mouth and moans around it.

His eyes close in rapture right before he pulls off again. Felix grips his own dick and jerks himself right over my face. I watch in awe as Felix's expert hand works his cock. "Enjoying the show?" he asks.

"I want to know what I can do for you –

I don't finish the sentence about how I'm watching so I can learn to touch them the way they want. Dex captures my cheeks in his hands and meets my eyes. His expression is wild, his eyes black holes I don't recognize. "I'm going to come deep inside of you and then Felix is going to clean you up again. Understand?"

What does he mean Felix is going to clean me again? I nod. What else can I do? Get up and leave?

Not happening. Mostly because I don't have any desire to leave this room. This bed.

He thrusts harder and faster and moves back to blowing Felix, who moans his own approval at being included. Dex laps, licks, and sucks Felix's cock and balls like he's exuberantly eating food after starving for weeks. Will I ever be that excited to have a man's cock in my mouth?

Guttural moans come from Dex's throat until he grips my hips and pushes into me to the hilt. His thrusts stop, but his shoulders tremble, and his cock twitches inside of me. When he withdraws, wetness dribbles from my most intimate place, and

I momentarily wonder if I peed myself before realizing it's Dex's release.

Dex moves back to his knees, keeps my thighs spread apart, and looks at Felix. "Snack time."

Seconds

Felix

Nicole scowls, and her eyes flick around the room, frowning. She doesn't understand the reference, and that's cute as hell.

She'll learn soon enough.

I move from my spot by her head and quickly crawl so that I'm next to Dex, both of us staring between her thighs like we're doctors consulting on a surgical procedure. The ridiculousness of it almost sends me over the edge with laughter before Dex places a simple kiss on my cheek and then brings his hand to the back of my head. He pushes me forward, and I chuckle at his exuberance as I lean into Nicole's spread legs and take a long lick up her slit. The salty, familiar taste of Dex's cum hits my tongue, and I pause to roll it around in my mouth before closing my lips over Nicole's pussy and sucking.

Dex whimpers at the slurping sound as I swallow his load and then lap at Nicole until every drop dribbling from her pussy is gone. Her legs tremble around my ears, and I hold her thighs open so I can lick and suck. She tries to hide, probably horrified that I'm eating my partner's cum from her most intimate place, but I can't get enough. I'm drunk on them both. I'm completely ruined by the taste of him mixed with her pleasure and the lingering metallic taste of her lost innocence.

"Good enough, Felix," Dex whispers, tapping my chin. "Show me."

Dutifully, I open my mouth and stick out my tongue, showing him that I swallowed every drop I could reach. I glance at Nicole and smile at her wide eyes and mouth open in an O shape. She blinks as she wraps her brain around what I just did.

"Nicole," Dex says, clearing his throat. It takes a few seconds, but she eventually breaks eye contact with me and looks at him. "Would you like to take care of Felix, or would you like to watch me do it?"

She bites her lip and looks at me, then Dex again, before she answers. "Two men?"

"I told you we do everything together," Dex answers. "But if you don't want him, are you OK if I take care of him now?"

Her eyes practically roll back in her head as Dex and I wait on our knees a few inches from her body. The heat of her skin practically scorches my own, and I long for the tight pussy in front of me. But I won't do it if the idea of two men inside of her little body in one night confuses or upsets her.

"What do you want, Dex?" she asks.

He lies on the bed next to her and strokes her hair. I'm wild with want for something – anything – against my dick. I'd bite through a chain for someone to touch me or let me put my cock somewhere. I tremble and wait patiently for Dex to tell me what he wants.

He nuzzles her throat and kisses her lips. She wraps her arm around his neck, grips his hair, and pulls him to her again.

All. While. I. Fucking. Wait.

I'm about ready to start fucking the blanket when Dex breaks their kiss and glances at me, only to notice my dark eyes and clenched jaw. "I want to watch Felix take you."

"I can have two men in one night?"

God, she can't really be that naïve.

"I didn't know that was possible to have that many...you knows...inside of me."

Scratch that. Apparently, it *is* possible for her to be so uneducated.

Dex leans down to her cheek and speaks against her skin. "I love watching him almost as much as when I get to fuck him or when he sucks me off. But I want you to lie on my chest while he fucks you from behind."

"From behind? Like in my butt?" she asks, frantic.

Dex and I both shake our heads. "No. He'll use your pussy. He'll just do it in a different position than what you've probably been taught men and women do. Did you grow up on a farm?"

"Not on one, but there was a farm nearby."

"So, you've seen dogs or other animals mate, right?" She nods, her eyes wide again. "There's a reason they call this position doggy style."

"What do I do?" Nicole asks, a tremble in her voice. Her cheeks are pink, probably with embarrassment, but I can tell she's desperate to please Dex. Her eyes track him at all times, and she doesn't let him get more than an inch away from her.

Dex lies back on the bed and adjusts the pillow under him. He pats his chest. "Roll over and put your face right here so you can be close to me."

She does as he asks, and a growl comes from my chest, hopeful that we'll get the show on the road here, and I can get relief.

"Put your ass in the air for Felix."

Nicole places her hands on the bed on either side of Dex and grips the blanket like she's scared. I'm so desperate to fuck the pink pussy now in my face, I don't care about her fucking feelings. Dex can comfort her. He's good at that. I can't think of anything but my insane desire. My heart pounds in my ears, and sweat drips down my neck.

Dex tilts Nicole's chin so their eyes meet. "Good girl. Felix is very good at what he does, so look at me while you enjoy it. I want to watch how good he makes you feel."

Dex looks at me and nods, which is my queue to have at it.

I run my hand down Nicole's back from the nape of her neck to her tailbone. She shakes under me and wiggles her butt a bit. On any other woman, I'd take that as enticement. On her, it's nerves.

When I reach the top of her butt crack, I bend down a little and spit on her ass before watching it drip down to her pussy. "I thought you needed a little extra lube here, sweetheart."

She whimpers, and Dex runs his hands through her hair. "You're so fucking beautiful. Look at me."

I grip her hips and massage them. She's so different from Dex. Hips. The curve of her waist is different. Even her smell is so feminine that I pause, full of want but unsure if I remember how to fuck a woman properly. It's been a while since Dex and I shared one, come to think of it.

But this isn't my first rodeo.

I roll my shoulders confidently, lest Dex thinks I'm not interested in sharing. Leaning forward, I kiss her earlobe and push my face into her neck as I slide into her waiting body. My eyes flutter at the feel of a silky pussy that's so different from an asshole. It's not as tight as ass, but it's softer. Wetter. With a natural warmth that's distinct and very much appreciated.

She's tight around me, and her body still trembles either from her last orgasm or fear.

I clear my throat. "Some men don't like sloppy seconds," I say, my voice husky as my cock trembles inside of her, begging to ravage the annoying little bitch. "But I like it. It's so wet, and I love his cum soaking my cock when I take a woman. I sucked most of it out, but I can still feel it," I practically hum.

She shivers at my words, but with Dex at her front and me at her back, I know she isn't shivering from the cold.

Her response empowers me. I fist a handful of long, brown hair and curl it around my hand. "Look at him."

"Huh?" she asks under me, her voice making it sound almost like a meow.

I yank on her just a bit. I don't want to hurt her in front of Dex. "Look at him. I want him to watch every expression as it passes over your face while I fuck you."

I hold on to her hair like it's a horse rein with one hand and control her hips with the other as I thrust into her. I close my eyes and throw my head back at the intensity and filth of it. Dex whispers and coos to her as she looks at him. He strokes her hair sweetly as I'm not so sweet to the other end.

Where Dex was kind and gentle with her, I'm urgent and, frankly, a dick. I take her hard, pushing into her like she's done this hundreds of times, not caring if she hates me.

But she doesn't hate me. She bucks back against me, and curse words spill from her mouth. When I lean to see her facial expression, I find a line of drool hanging from her mouth as I pound into her.

"That's it. Take it. Take all of me." I yank on her hair a little. "I don't think you're as innocent as you act because you like what I'm giving you, don't you, Nicole?"

She doesn't answer, so I spank her bottom. A yelp comes from her mouth, but she swivels her hips up and against me.

I laugh. I laugh as I fuck Dex's perfect angel. I'm not sold on her, and I don't know if I ever will be, but she likes to fuck, and she likes it hard. Who knew?

"I love watching you give yourself to Felix, sweetheart. Fuck, you're so sexy and beautiful right now. So wild."

Whimpers and mews come from her mouth as I take her again and again. When I get close, I still for a moment, swivel my cock inside of her, and smack her only to watch my red handprint bloom on her butt cheek.

I'm not a complete beast, though. The rosy mark is too much for me to bear, and I massage the red out of her creamy skin. She sighs every time I massage her ass. The little bitch is liking everything I give her no matter how hard or how filthy I talk to her.

Eventually, I can't stop my release. My balls contract as electric shockwaves move up my back and then down to my toes. My head falls back, my mouth opens, and I moan Dex's name as I unload my balls inside the woman he's starting to love. I know, from the look on his face, that it's love because I haven't seen that look on him since the day we met.

Dance with Me

Dex...Two Weeks Later

"**Y**ou really want to buy this place someday?" Nicole asks as soon as we're at the door.

I smile a little as the bouncer doesn't even check her ID this time. First, she's with me, and that's good enough for Ralph. Second, she's been here twice with me, and the door people make a note of who comes and goes with me so they don't hassle my friends. Felix hasn't waited in line to get into a club since 1975, and Nicole won't wait at any club in a twenty-block radius for the rest of her life.

"I sure do," I say next to her ear.

I press my hand on her back and nudge her through the packed room. Looking around, I try to see it through her eyes. It's loud and has the distinct disco club vibe of somehow being both dim and bright at the same time. It's bright in places, and those places change with every turn of the ball as it casts light in a strobe effect through the room. I inhale deeply and wrinkle my nose at the scent of body odor, sweat, liquor, and the subtle undertone of sex that happens in the booths despite it being public. I'm used to the smell, so it doesn't bother me, but I wonder if the smell of a bar disgusts her. To me, the particular club that has changed hands and names several times over the years has the same effect as some people probably have with coming home to their mother and smelling fresh laundry and homemade beef stew.

The hostess, Karma, approaches me as soon as she finds me. I'm not sure if it's her real name, but that's all we've ever called her. Nicole stiffens at my side as the beautiful woman who looks like a disco goddess licks her lips as she looks me up and down. Where Nicole is soft, Karma is hard with her cut cheekbones and over-arched eyebrows. Long, blonde hair that's obviously ironed hangs past her ass, and her pink sequined leisure suit reflects the disco ball's light so that I damn near have to shield my eyes.

"Usual booth, Mr. Holden?" Karma asks, and I silently plead with my eyes that she not come on to me or spill the beans that Karma's joined Felix and me in a booth more than once. It's been a while since that's happened, and I worry she'll roll the dice tonight.

"Yes, please. And drinks for us. My usual. Extra olives this time, though. Nicole will have a Shirley Temple. Keep them coming." I hand her a small wad of ten-dollar bills, and she palms them. Thankfully, she doesn't judge Nicole for the Shirley Temple.

"Your pill of choice tonight?"

Nicole turns to me with a quizzical expression. Fuck.

"No disco biscuits tonight," I chuckle, trying to laugh it off as a ridiculous question. "I only indulge if Felix and I are celebrating and want to relax. Nic doesn't do drugs, so please don't bring them or offer when she's with me."

Karma looks over my shoulder like she suddenly realizes Felix isn't on my arm. She turns her eyes back to Nicole, looking her up and down with an expression that I can practically read. She probably wonders if Nicole is my sister or cousin and certainly wonders why I'm with her. Nicole is stunning in the tight miniskirt I bought her when we were shopping the other day. She walked up to it and stared at the window until I insisted she let me get it for her. Even in a miniskirt and her new post earrings that shimmer in the light, she still doesn't look like a woman who's been hardened by liquor, drugs, and too many nights of dancing. There's certainly a look of the club girls, and Nicole isn't it. It's one of the things I like about her. If I wanted a disco ho, I'd get a disco ho.

A look of disdain crosses Karma's face, and I clench my fists in silent frustration for Nicole. "Nicole is my girlfriend. Felix is my partner. Everyone is aware of everything. I won't explain further, but Nicole needs to be cared for like I'm with her at all times, even if I'm not. She has access to my booth and my bar tab every time she's here. Same as Felix. Clear?"

"Yes, Mr. Holden. Will there be anything else?"

I look around the packed club and find Daniel McCallister across the room, one arm around a blonde woman while a man of about Nicole's age bobs his head over Daniel's lap. Nicole follows my eyes, cringes, and I squeeze her hand.

"Send Daniel a line for me." I hand Karma more cash before she nods and turns to leave.

"Is that guy getting sucked by that other man?" Nicole asks, waving her hand over my genital area as soon as Karma's out of earshot.

I laugh at her inability to ask what he's doing out loud. "Yep. That's Daniel. He's the current owner, and the person I have to butter up to come down in price if I ever want to own this place. That's a year or so down the road after another location turns a profit, but I still like to make him happy when I can." I turn to face her and slide my hand around her waist. "Like I said when we met, I don't do cocaine, but I will certainly gift it if it greases the wheels to get this club. I can stop if it upsets you. Do you want me to stop the ludes too? Because I will if it bothers you. I'm getting too old for this shit anyway."

Nicole looks at the disco ball as another song comes on, but she ignores my question. I know this is still a different world for her, so I quietly lead her to the booth I usually sit in if I want to have a simple drink and watch the dance floor.

"You really need to win, huh?" she asks once we're seated.

I bite my lip and scowl. "Win what?"

"The contest," Nicole says, and I quickly nod, realizing what she means. "You need to win so you can get your second location and eventually buy the disco."

I look around the club. It feels like home and is no more impressive to me now than my own living room. "I've wanted to own it since I first came here. That was back when I hadn't met Felix yet. A long time ago."

"Does Daniel know you want it?" she asks, leaning in so I can hear her over the loud music.

I nod and smile as a waitress sets our drinks down before sashaying over to Daniel to take him his cocaine. The waitress points over to Nicole and me, and Daniel raises his glass in cheers. I raise my martini back at him before looking at Nicole. "Yes, he knows. He's biding his time until he hits retirement age. We talked about it a few months ago. He's got a couple more years here and then wants to buy a boat and a house on Lake Geneva. There's a line for people who want to buy it, but I think he likes me the best. I just want to have enough money in the bank to pull the trigger when he says he's ready to sell. As long as I grease him with coke and send women over, he'll give me the first swing at a bid. I know him well enough for that."

She looks down and takes a drink of her Shirley Temple. "That's a lot of pressure. Are you sure I'm the right person for the job?"

I lean forward as far as I can get with the table between us and tilt her chin to look me in the eye. "It's too late now if you're the wrong girl. I can't train someone else in such a short time, and you're doing wonderfully." My eyes flick to the dance floor as "Disco Inferno" comes over the sound system. "Do you want to prove it?"

Nicole nearly sputters her drink. "Prove it?"

"Dance with me."

"Now? Here?"

"We're at a disco bar, Nicole."

She rolls her shoulders. "But we just got our drinks. Who's going to watch them?"

I look around the crowded room and spot a bouncer I know, catching his eye. I point to our drinks and then at the dance floor in a silent signal to make sure no one fucks with them. "Nobody will touch our drinks or the booth. Trust me."

"Are you sure you don't already own a part of this place?"

I laugh and slide out of the booth to offer her my hand. "Not yet, baby, but you're going to help me make that happen someday."

She puts her hand in mine, and I kiss the top of it, a move so old-fashioned that it looks like it could have come straight out of a silent movie. We walk together to the dance floor, where the crowd parts like it usually does when it sees me. Greetings by my name fill my ears, and hands are held up for me to high-five.

Nicole looks like she did the first couple of times she was here with me. Uneasy. The first time she was here was when we met. The second time, she sat at the bar on a thinned-out Tuesday and watched me work the room before we went to dinner. That was weeks ago, though.

This is the first time on the dance floor with me since the night we met, and I'm going to show her off.

"Are we going through our routine?" she asks as she stands so close to me her breasts are squeezed against my arm. Not that I mind. I quite enjoy her breasts anywhere on me that she wants to put them.

"No, sweetheart. We're just going to have fun." I let go of her hand and face her as people make room for us on the dance floor. They know me and know to give me space. "Have fun with me. Remember what I told you the night we met?"

"That you like virgins?" she teases.

I lean forward until I'm next to her ear before placing a single kiss on the lobe. "That too. But I was referring to disco being something you take your time with. It's just for fun, outside of a very serious contest in a few weeks."

She closes her eyes, willing herself to start moving, and I wrap one arm around her waist. "Dance with me, Nicole."

Her eyes stay closed as she rocks into the music, letting me lead her. Nobody cares that her eyes are closed. Most of the people in the club have hazy, glassy, or heavy-lidded eyes from drugs every night anyway, but Nicole's eyes are closed in rapture.

I pull her closer as the tempo picks up, and we gyrate together. She bucks awkwardly a few times but soon matches my rhythm. I don't shake it up like I would if I danced with Felix or another experienced disco dancer. I do a few movements Nicole can catch, and then we move around the dance floor, a blur of shoulders, legs, and hips. The lighting changes colors from blues to reds and then to yellows over us, and the colors bounce off Nicole's skin, giving her the appearance of a woman who belongs here – belongs with me.

I lean forward and find her mouth with my own as the song changes to "Take a Chance on Me," and the song is fitting since I wish Felix was here to listen to the message, only to take a chance on Nicole.

Nicole and I do some twists and passes under my arms. I dip her into the rhythm, and by the end of the song, she's laughing like it's great fun. People look her up and down appreciatively, and when some other men get close, I pull her close to me as our chests shimmy together to the music. I may be willing to share her with Felix because he's also the love of my life, but my jealous side rears its head when other men look at her.

Mine.

Mine and Felix's if he'll ever come around and admit she'd be good for him.

I want to scream it – point at her and make sure everyone in this damn club knows she's with me.

I turn her once more and let her twist under my arms as she laughs. When she's righted again, she wraps her arms around my trunk and runs her hand up my back. "Will it always be like this?" she asks, disco lights dancing in her eyes.

I push the bridge of my nose against hers. "I'll make it like this as long as you let me, Nicole."

We don't go back to the booth. Screw the drinks. Screw everything, including the nosy eyes as I lead Nicole to the side of the bar and down the hall to the restrooms. At the T in the hall before the bathrooms, I pull her into a cove only the barbacks use and gently push her against the old, brick wall, burying my face in her neck.

She laughs and pushes against me as I nip and lick at the skin of her throat. "Someone will see."

I run my hands up her thigh and under her skirt. "Nobody will care. It's novel we're attempting to hide it."

"Here?"

I nod and nip at her chin. "Here. Just you and me. Against this wall like the big girls do it, Nicole. Is that why you wore this little skirt? For me to lift it up, slide my hands in those panties, and take you the way I know you now like right here in the club?"

She smiles against my cheek. "How do you know I like it?"

"The sounds you made when I made you come. When Felix fucked you hard. All you have to do is lift your leg or wrap them around me and let me make you feel good again."

Her chest heaves, and she buries her face in my neck, inhaling my scent deeply as I work her skirt up with my hands. I run a single finger over her basic, white panties with a single pink rose embroidered at the waistband. When I get to the rose, I twirl it in my fingers. "So innocent still, even though Felix and I took you again and again that night. So different from what I've had before. Perfection."

She hums into my skin, and then those gloriously long legs wrap around my waist as I push aside the embroidered under-

wear, close my eyes, and sink into the woman I want as much as
I want Felix.

Kneed Me

Felix

A shrill sound pulls me from my sleep, and I slap at the alarm clock next to our bed. "Dex!" I yell, hoping he can reach it better. "Turn it off."

The sound is relentless, and I squint at the snooze button on the alarm clock. I'm sure I hit the damn thing. It takes me a few moments as my brain turns on to realize it's three in the afternoon and not the alarm clock making the noise. Stumbling from the bed and untangling my legs from the sheets bunched at my ankles, I amble toward the living room and the phone on the end table. The caller's not giving up. The damn thing has been ringing for a couple minutes by the time I reach it.

"Felix," I grunt instead of a normal greeting.

"F-Felix? It's Nicole."

"Oh, hello." I pinch my nose in irritation and put my hand on my hip. I swallow to keep my words in check. No use being mean to her because she woke me from a nap. It's certainly not the first time I'll play secretary for her and give a message to Dex. "Dex isn't here. He's at the studio." My foggy brain whirls, and I put pieces together in my mind. "Wait, aren't you with him at the studio? Did you not go to work today?"

"You need to come to Mercy General. He fell, and he's being examined." She sniffles as cold fear moves up my spine.

"What the hell do you mean he fell? Off a ladder or something?"

She sobs, and I wave my hands at the phone like I'm willing her to speak. "He was teaching a tango class. One of the ladies came out and said he fell while doing a turn. Can you just come down here, Felix? I don't know what to do, and they won't let me back there yet."

My breathing is choppy, and I drop the phone on the floor as I sprint for the bedroom to grab some pants suitable for a hospital visit. I quickly run my hand through my hair, making it presentable enough for the public. I grab the keys off the hook and hear Nicole's voice from far away, yelling for me. It's only then that I realize I didn't hang up the phone. I simply dropped it.

I run to the phone, pick it up, and hold it to my ear to listen to a sobbing Nicole. "I'm coming, Nic. I'll be there in ten minutes. Just hang on and wait for me in the waiting room."

I hang it up this time and bolt out the door, only taking the time to lock the knob part. I chuckle to myself since I'm the guy who insists on the deadbolt being locked every time someone isn't here. Dex would rib me if he was here to witness this.

I don't wait for the elevator, and I sprint down the stairs as fast as my legs can take me. Thankfully, a cab has its light on outside the building, and I quickly get in and give the directions to the hospital. The man must hear the urgency in my voice because I'm at the hospital in eight minutes and shoving a wad of cash in his face, surely overtipping the man.

As soon as the doors to the emergency area open, I spot Nicole standing near the payphone and watching the door. Tears run down her face, smearing her mascara, and she shivers in the cold waiting room with only her tank top on. She straightens when she sees me and crosses the room in only a few strides. Without thinking much about it, I wrap her in my arms and pull her to my chest. "Shhh," I coo. "What happened?"

"He twisted it when he did a turn. That's what Betty Freeburg said," she says. "He was in so much pain I could hardly talk to him to get his version. A couple of the stronger men got him in a cab, and I brought him here. Will they talk to you?"

I pull away from her but keep my hand on her back. "They're actually more likely to talk to you in case you're his girlfriend or wife."

"But you're his partn – Oh."

I nod and smirk. "Welcome to our world. Did they even ask who you are to him?"

She shakes her head. "They said they'd check him and come out later."

I roll my shoulders with annoyance at the situation. For the first time, I'm in the same room as Nicole and not annoyed at her. In fact, I'm glad she's here. I'm relieved she was with Dex and took care of him. Will this be what it's like if I ever accept her into our relationship – or accept anyone Dex and I decide to love together? Is this what teamwork in a relationship between more than two people feels like?

"When they come back, I'm his brother and you're his wife. Got it?"

She nods. "I'll lie."

I can't help it, I snort. "Yes, you can lie in this case."

She blows out a breath and wraps her arms back around my waist. I'm too emotionally wrecked to think twice about it. Actually, her head feels good on my chest, like it's holding my heart in my chest cavity. I prop my chin on her head and hug her back. When I look down, her eyes are closed like she's sleeping.

"I'm sure he'll be OK. When you said he fell, I imagined a head wound or something."

"I'm sorry I scared you, Felix," she says, wiping her nose.

I push my face into her hair because my body doesn't know what else to do. "Thanks for calling me, and thanks for making sure he was safe before taking the time to dial. You did the right thing."

"I'm looking for Dex Holden's wife," an older nurse with steel gray hair calls from the nurse's station.

I pull away from Nicole and point at her. "Right here."

"You can come back and see him now," the nurse says, waving Nicole around the station entrance.

Nicole takes a few steps and stops. "Can his brother come back?" she asks, meeting my eyes.

"Only one person. Are you his wife? He said his wife was out here when we asked. If you're not his wife, you'll have to stay –

"Go ahead, Sis," I say, interrupting the nurse. Dex obviously knew they wouldn't let anyone but his spouse back, and that won't be me any time soon. "My *brother* needs you." I widen my eyes at Nicole, willing her to understand she should just go the hell back there. "I'll get us some of those yummy-looking cups of hospital coffee. Nothing but the best for my favorite sister-in-law. I'll be here when you get done."

She gives a short nod and walks to the nurse's station to listen to the directions of where she's supposed to go. The woman who's known Dex for all of a couple months walks away, looking back and waving once, as I slouch into a plastic chair and wait for the man I've known for years to be OK enough for me to see him.

***

"No!" I say, shaking my head. "Absolutely fucking not. No way. No how. Get it out of your head."

Nicole is in the hall bathroom, and Dex has his leg propped on the coffee table, an ice pack on top of his bandaged knee.

Crutches are nearby, and a prescription for a painkiller I've never heard of is scrawled on a doctor's note nearby. Another piece of paper is under it, but I don't want to talk about it or hear about it. I want all of this to go away.

"Felix, you're my only hope here." His voice is low. Defeated.

I pick up the prescription note, fold it, and shove it into my pants pocket. "I'll go get this prescription filled, and when I come back, I expect you to have a different solution." I whisper it, but it sounds like hissing. I don't want Nicole to hear.

"Do it for me."

God damn him and the words he knows work on me. He knows that requesting I do something for him will twist the knife and render me powerless.

His face scrunches in anguish, and his chin quivers. I cannot and will not watch this man cry unless it's from intense knee pain. That's the only acceptable crying I will allow at this point. He will not cry over that dance contest and the fact that the other paper in his hand is an order to not do anything requiring twisting or making sudden turns for six weeks.

The contest is in three.

Hell, he'll be on crutches for the next two. Not only is he asking me to take over the contest, but I'm also going to have a full schedule at the studio when I pick up his classes. Dex is even making me teach Nicole the damn waltz so she can help with classes.

"I can't do it," I say.

"You'll have to be a strong lead," he says, his jaw set like he's chastising a child.

"Why? Because she sucks?" I whisper, jerking my thumb over my shoulder in the direction of the bathroom.

"She doesn't suck. She has it down. She'll only struggle with confidence. You have three weeks to practice. It'll be enough. You know the routine. For fuck's sake, you helped me choreograph it."

I shake my head. "No. No. No. Then some more no. I do not want to spend three weeks training my partner's insufferable girlfriend for a dance contest."

He looks down and inhales. I know that sound. He does it when he's annoyed with me and needs space. Tough. I'm not giving it to him.

"This is for all of us, Felix.," he says. "We talked about this. I can hire more staff, and we can expand. I told you the current studio is yours once I get my own location. Don't you want that? Don't you want to be able to buy the club after both locations take off?"

I bring my hands to my neck, clasping my fingers as I look at the ceiling. "I'd be spending hours with her a day. I'm not ready for that."

"Why?"

"You can't be serious." I lean back a little to check to be sure Nicole isn't listening in the hallway.

"Maybe if you spent time with her like I spend time with her, you'd like her more."

"Or I could hate her more."

Dex laughs like he's watching Carson. "It's not possible to hate her. She's too sweet. She may annoy you with her innocence, but you don't hate her. Admit it."

I roll my shoulders and purse my lips. I know I'm acting like a teenager, but he's right. I don't hate her. I just see her as a rival for Dex's affection and someone I wouldn't normally hang out with but have to hang out with on some level. But hours of dance training a day? Fuck off.

"Felix?" Dex chides.

"OK, I don't hate her. She's just an acquired taste for me, and I haven't acquired her taste yet."

"You made love to her like you meant it a few weeks ago."

I walk closer to him, and he looks up at me from his seated position. I grip his hair roughly and won't let him look away. "That was for you."

"Bullshit. I saw the way you touched her. Don't piss on me and tell me it's raining. You forget I know you. You can deny it all you want, but I see you, Felix. Put your pride aside for not being the one to pick her because, here's the rub, I think you would have picked her if she had just been our secretary first and not my love interest." He glares at me without blinking. "If she had come in off the street and worked for us as our sweet, innocent assistant, you would have eventually seen something in her, Felix."

"You don't know that."

"And this would be for me, too."

"You're calling in a lot of favors, Dex. When is it about me? When do I have a say?"

"Talking about me?" a voice asks.

Dex leans to look around my body and smiles. I cringe before turning around to face Nicole. "Yeah, we were. We were talking about the contest. Dex can't do it. It'll have to be me." I run my hand through my hair in frustration, and a low growl comes from my chest. "Well, Dex *wants* it to be me."

Nicole looks at Dex's wrapped knee and takes a deep breath. "I kind of figured the contest was off."

The damn clock Dex insists on keeping ticks in the corner, and I *feel* Dex's eyes burning a hole in my back. His judgment burns my skin from behind. Even worse, I can practically smell the disappointment wafting from Nicole's pores.

I hate it.

What the hell is wrong with me? If there's no contest, she's just Dex's coworker and part-time lover. If he doesn't have a reason to spend tons of time with her, maybe he won't.

But I hate disappointing her, to say nothing of letting down Dex when he needs me.

This is my golden opportunity to get rid of her and be Dex's hero again. If I don't enter this contest with her, it'll turn her into our simple secretary and coffee maker for our elderly students. Dex will get bored, I'll demand more time with him, and she'll slide out of his life soon enough.

So, why can't I pull the trigger?

She watches me with her bright green eyes, and my fingers flex because I have half a mind to cup her cheeks and take her to our room like Dex and I did a few weeks ago.

Is Dex right? Am I starting to like her or at least tolerate her?

She steps closer to me and puts her hand in the center of my chest just as my heart starts to pound harder. Can she feel it? If so, does she know the reaction is because she's so close to me now?

"Felix, will you be my dance partner so we can win that contest for Dex?"

Dex makes a humming sound at the sweetness of her request. I haven't seen a woman this vulnerable since Janice Meekum asked me to dance at the ninth-grade sock hop. Just like Janice, Nicole's eyes are wide and the slightest bit watery, like she's holding in tears. Her voice is low and unsure of itself, and I realize that's what infuriates me the most about her. I demand she have confidence if I have to be around her. I want someone brazen enough to put me in my place and bold enough to be her own person. If she's neither of those things, she won't keep Dex's interest, and I'm scared to get attached if she's going to be gone soon anyway. I just don't see any confidence from her yet.

I open my mouth to say so when Dex taps me on the butt. I roll my eyes, and I'm sure Nicole thinks I'm rolling them at her. "Ugh," I say. Nicole steps back because she must think I'm growling at her. "Fine. We can start when I get back from filling King Dex's prescription."

Dropped

Nicole

"Again," Felix practically growls. The hair on the back of my neck stands at attention, and my stomach drops. I know he won't hit me, but he sounds angry and irritated.

"I'm doing the best I can."

He scoffs and walks to the record player to start the music again while I adjust the black bodysuit Dex bought me for practice. I guess he was tired of me complaining about my clothes being uncomfortable and not disco-inspired. It's hard to disco when you don't look like disco.

It's been almost a full week of constant training with Felix, and it has been...not fun. He grunts whenever I do the thigh sit, like my one-hundred-and-ten-pound frame is too much for him, or he picks apart every single maneuver I do. When I dare ask him why he's being so picky, he barks at me about not half-assing this performance, and he's not going to coddle me to save my sensitive little feelings.

I know he's annoyed, but I'm also frustrated beyond belief – partly because he's right, and I don't want to admit it. I can't half-ass this if we want to win.

I run my eyes up Felix's body as he drinks from his cup of water on the table. His pants couldn't be any tighter, and I have to peel my eyes away from the front of his trousers. When he turns around to get a towel for his face, I don't restrain myself from checking out his ass. He may be in a jerk mood, but I lick my lips at the idea of just reaching out and cupping his...

The needle scratching across the record interrupts my thoughts of Felix's ass. He hurries back to me and pushes his forehead to mine in the start position. "Get it right this time," he mutters. "We have two weeks."

We move together in perfect unison for the first part of the song and break into our behind-the-neck hand sequence. Felix hisses when I don't bend my elbow, but I quickly pick up the rest of the sequence and execute it flawlessly. He picks me up, and I sit on his thigh for a moment as he dips me before putting me into a single spin around him. He dips me again as we look at each other like we're in love.

Well, we're *supposed* to look at each other like we're in love. I smile at Felix. He glowers at me.

"Move," he grunts. "You're like a sack of flour today, Nicole."

We move into a complicated footwork sequence, the one I've been showing Dex every single night whether Felix is there and staring at me or not. Dex thinks I'm making improvement, but Felix picks apart every step. This time, I do it flawlessly, and I smile to myself as I move in front of Felix to do a trust fall.

I'm supposed to fall back, and he's *supposed* to catch me under my armpits. I fall back, but Felix doesn't catch me. My ass hits the floor, and I fall all the way onto my back, hitting my head against the soft wood in the process.

"What the hell, Felix?"

"Don't nag me. God, Dex should have taught you how to fall properly."

I squint from my spot on the floor. He has to be screwing with me. "How does one fall properly?"

"Gracefully with a little roll," Felix says. He smiles like he's on the verge of laughter, and he makes a rolling motion with his hands. To finish it off, he does a jazz-hands movement.

I can't speak. Felix doesn't help me off the floor. He just walks to the record player and watches until I get up, rubbing my sore ass.

"You could say you're sorry."

He smiles a sarcastic grin. "But I'm not, sweetheart. You have to learn to do things properly."

"You dropped me on purpose."

"Why would I do that?"

"Come on."

He looks at me and sets his jaw. "Prove it."

I roll my shoulders and set my own jaw. I don't glare at Felix often, but he's pressing my buttons. I thought we were getting along better. Sure, we haven't been physical since the night Dex took my virginity, but we've danced together, hugged in the hospital, and I've even made the bastard laugh a few times – and not at my expense.

"Again," he says, hurrying into position.

He presses his forehead to mine, and our eyes connect. Something breaks then. Maybe it's me glaring back at him. Maybe he's realized he's been an insufferable asshole. Maybe it's just our touching. Whatever it is, his eyes soften for a moment, and I know all my problems with him amount to one big pissing contest. So much is communicated in that look. He doesn't *want* to be mean to me. Somewhere deep inside Felix is a nice person. It's the jealousy that eats at him, and it's suddenly so clear.

He has to prove to the world he's better than me. More importantly, he's trying to prove it to Dex.

I'm not going to let him win. He may have a piece of Dex's heart, but I won't let him make me feel like crap.

I blink and start my routine in perfect tandem with him as the music starts. He grunts a sound like *huh* when I nail my foot sequence this time, and he doesn't even grunt when I do the thigh sit.

I turn and start the sequence into the trust fall, and I brace for it this time. I know he missed on purpose before, and part of me *knows* he'll do it again. I know he has better hand-eye coordination than to miss my armpits twice.

He expects fear. He wants me to turn and look or falter before the fall so he can say I'm hesitating – that I'm screwing up the routine. He wants to go home and tell Dex I'm not confident.

I won't give him the satisfaction. He gets everything. He got Dex first. He has Dex's ear. He has a stake in Dex's business. He will not get my pride or my trusting nature. I also have a hunch that the surest way to put him in his place is to not play his game.

I blindly fall back, and he misses...again.

My ass hits the ground with a grunt. This time, I don't look at Felix or even turn around. I didn't fall all the way down. I sit for a moment, blow out a breath, and get up like I'm just getting up after I had a nice picnic on a warm sunny day.

He holds out his hand like he's making an effort, and I ignore it. "Start the music again, Felix," I say, dusting off my black leotard.

He stalks back to the record player and starts the music again. We move through the routine and get to the trust fall this time. Expecting it again, he doesn't drop me this time, but the next lift is a jump into him. I'm supposed to jump, he catches me, and then I slide down his body before he catches my hands, pulling me up from the floor.

I jump.

I slide.

I lean back.

He misses my hand.

My eyes widen, and my mouth opens when I realize I'll hit the ground in another millisecond. He puts his hands on his hips and bends over me as I'm sprawled on the floor. "Who has bad hand-eye coordination? Seriously, Nicole, catch my damn hand next time."

I giggle. I can't help it. It's not my normal laugh, and it sounds downright maniacal. This jerk actually thinks he's going to get rid of me by dropping me. I laugh so hard that I clap my hands like Felix is the funniest man on the planet. He even takes two steps away and furrows his brow like he's watching me finally snap.

Eventually, I stand and grit my teeth, then remember I shouldn't let him see that he's getting to me.

"Looks like you had an accident there," I taunt.

"Me?" he scoffs. "I'm the pro here, Nicole."

"My mistake. We can try again."

He saunters over to the record player once again, a smirk creasing his face, and I have the urge to smack it right off him. A scream sticks in my throat because I want to lash out and rage at him that I'm doing my best. I'm doing all of this for the man we both have feelings for. This is for Dex. Not for my ego. Not for Felix. If this was about Felix, I'd already be out the door the first time he dropped me.

Dex said to stay calm and Felix would show who he really is.

Is he really an asshole that drops me the first time Dex isn't looking? Is he looking for the first opportunity to run to Dex and tell him I'm an unhinged shrew with an anger issue?

That's exactly what would happen.

I set my shoulders and smile as he quickly returns. When he presses his forehead to mine this time, we glare at each other, both of us grinning wry smiles like we refuse to let the other get the better of us. Something hums between us, and if I wasn't so damn angry with him for dropping me, I'd press my lips against his and see what he tastes like.

We do the routine flawlessly, and he doesn't drop me this time. I get so confident that he won't drop me, that I miss steps in the side-by-side footwork sequence that sends him stomping to the record player, seething in silence.

"Sorry," I say, meaning it. He got so in my head, I was waiting for the other shoe to drop.

He doesn't acknowledge my apology. He only stomps back over to me in such an un-Felix-like way that he makes me take a few steps back until he wraps his arm around my waist and drags me to the center of the floor.

"I told you before. I'll never hurt you," he seethes.

"Liar. You dropped me."

"Accidents."

"Bullshit," I say with a smile as the music starts.

We move into the behind-the-neck hand movements and spin. When it comes time for the trust fall, I fall back without looking for him, only to land on my ass.

I fall all the way back since I was expecting him to catch me like he did the time before. When I look up, I find him leaning over me, his brow scrunched with fake concern. "Oops. Sorry."

I push off the floor, pull my shoulders back, and look him in the eye. I'm about to let him have it when I notice something. His head is tilted, and his eyes are soft. The space between his eyebrows is crinkled like he's upset or lost in sudden thought.

I turn away from him so I won't look at him anymore.

I clear my throat. "Again, Felix. I won't stop until you stop fucking up."

True Love

Dex

"It's a four-count here, right?" Nicole asks, turning in place and pantomiming the arm movements for the complex around-the-neck arm movements she performs in perfect unison with Felix before a gorgeous spin.

She's been practicing alone for me since Felix is at the studio teaching a waltz class to a busload of senior citizens we get every Wednesday afternoon from the local center. Surprisingly, practicing alone improves her hand and footwork sequences. I've never known that to happen since most dancers need a partner to set the rhythm. I did the right thing by trusting my instincts when I picked her up. She has natural talent she just needed to find, and Felix and I have molded her into a dancer.

Wanting to get up and dance with her, I sigh from my place on the couch and adjust the wrap on my knee. Felix always wraps it way too tight.

"You have that down. You have the whole thing down. It's perfect, Nicole."

She stops and slumps her shoulders forward.

"What is it?" I ask.

"Felix hates me. But even after all of that, I don't want to disappoint him."

"He doesn't hate you. We've been over this. If he hated you, he wouldn't have cared about your enjoyment when we were all together that one time and he wouldn't speak civilly to you at work. He's just...complicated."

"He's a dick sometimes, you know?"

"I see that, and I'm trying with him. I'm giving him space for things to happen on their own. I love you, Nicole." It rolls off my tongue so naturally that I don't even blink when I say it. She raises her head and looks at me. I hold my hands up. "Don't say it back if you don't mean it. I just wanted you to know how I feel because I want to keep you in my life. I love Felix so much, but I love you. I know I keep saying it, and I know it's hard, but he doesn't hate you. I can tell."

Nicole walks to the couch and lifts the heating pad that's nearby to check it's on before placing it over my knee. "I've never been in love Dex. Is this what it is?"

"What do you feel for me?" I ask.

I'm fully aware of ripping my heart open and laying it bare for her to stomp on if she doesn't feel the same way. If she's going to stick around, I need to know her motivation. Does she do this because I'm her boss and she's scared she'll be fired if she doesn't date me? The thought has been in the back of my mind since I started seeing something called sexual harassment cases on the news. The first case was brought a couple of years ago, but it just hit me that Nicole may feel coerced into sleeping with me after more cases have happened in Chicago.

After the heating pad is on my leg, she curls into my armpit and nestles her head under my chin. If she's being coerced, she's a damn good actress. "Is love when you'd do anything for someone?" she asks.

"Yes."

"Like enter a dance contest?"

I laugh into her hair before kissing the crown of her head. "Yes."

"Why do you love me, Dex?" Her voice is low when she asks it, and I strain my ears since the sound is muffled in my shirt.

"I thought you were the most innocent being I've ever met. I know you're the kindest person in my world. You work so hard for us. You're there when I need you, and you make me want to be there for all your needs. You give and then you let me give to you. You're also beautiful, and I just feel like we click. It's been that way for the last few months."

"Like love at first sight?" she asks, running her hand up my leg in a way that gets my dick's attention. "Does that exist?"

"I loved Felix at first sight. He loved me at first sight. It does exist." I run my hands through her hair as she traces her index finger over my hardening erection, and I smile at my innocent, little virgin now a minx when we're alone. "But you asked how I know, and I know I love you because I don't want to be away from you."

"You like me working for you? I'm worried about that – that I spend too much time with you."

"I come home from work and wish you were at dinner with me and Felix. When I go out with you, I wish Felix was there with his sarcastic comments and jaded commentary to counter your sunny disposition. I didn't realize how much I need your sun to Felix's rain until I met you. Now, I feel like the luckiest man alive because I get to have both of you in my life." I kiss her forehead as she looks up at me with doe eyes. "If I could, I'd snap my fingers so that Felix would love you like I do, but I know he needs time. It can't be instantaneous for everyone here. That's not realistic."

Nicole nods. "When I was growing up, I was told I may not love my husband at first but I'd grow to love him. I was told I should look for someone who would be a good provider and was from a nice family. I don't know why, but that made me not trust my feelings when I liked a boy."

"Did you have a high school boyfriend?"

She shakes her head. "I liked someone once. His name was David. I wasn't allowed to see him because his mother was a single mom. His dad had left as soon as his mother found out she was pregnant. There were lots of rumors about her. You know the type of things people say in small towns about single mothers." I nod into her hair. "Anyway, I always liked talking to him, and he'd throw rocks at my window some nights. Just to talk. Nothing scandalous happened. I mean, obviously." She waves her hand at her own crotch, probably reminding me she was a virgin until Felix and I took care of that.

"I'm invested in this. What happened?" I ask, propping my chin on my elbow and smiling that she's talking about something in her past.

"Nothing. We talked. I'd pine to see him on days when he wasn't at school. He worked a lot to help his mom, and he was too tired for school some days. Everyone looked down on him for it. He was great at art. I remember he'd draw me pictures. I think I still have some in a trunk under my bed." She snorts through her nose a little. "But Mom disapproved, so I could never date him or explore my feelings. It's such an old-fashioned idea to have now that I think about it. She said he would try to get me to do inappropriate things and wouldn't be a good provider. She said he was like his father and would impregnate me and run off. Maybe that's why I left town eventually. Mom was trying to set me up with her podiatrist's son. He was getting ready to finish his own podiatry program and coming home to wife shop."

"Nicole, I have a very serious question." She looks up at me, eyebrows creased. "Are you going to leave me for a second-generation podiatrist?"

She leans forward and kisses me on my chin. "Never. Because I think I love you, Dex Holden."

"Really?" My heart pounds so hard I wonder if she hears it.

She pulls back and holds up her hand to tick items off. "I can't wait to see you every single day. I can't wait to tell you things that happen to me because I feel like we're a team. I don't like being away from you, either, and I think I can trust you with my thoughts and feelings. It's like I can tell you anything. I also want to see where the future goes with you. That's love, right?"

"Throw in a hell of a sex life, and I think you nailed it."

"Sex life, huh?" she says, moving her attention back to my dick.

"And I have a theory about Felix. I've thought about it a lot, but I've never told him my thoughts."

She raises her head a little, enough to turn her ear to hear me better, her interest piqued. "A theory?"

"He likes that you're not easy for him."

A grunt comes out of her, and it's such an un-Nicole-like sound. "He likes that he hates me?"

"Like I said, he doesn't hate you. He likes that it's difficult with you. He's never had that, so he's confused. It's the thrill of the chase for him, but he doesn't recognize this as a chase. He wants it to be, but I delivered you to our apartment in the middle of the night on a silver platter. Maybe, deep down in his soul, Felix doesn't want love at first sight the next time love comes for him. He wants growth. He wants to try. So far, he hasn't had to try."

"That's an interesting theory." She rests her head back on my chest and moves back to fingering my cock through my pants. "But it's also bullshit. Nothing I've seen from him indicates he wants to try at all with me."

Nicole's hand moves to the button on my pants and soon works it free, but I scoot to the edge of the couch. I take her hand in mine, and she knows that's my hint for us to move to the bedroom. We've done this a few times now. I'm growing as comfortable with her body and tells as I am with Felix.

"I'm nervous about what Felix will think if I screw up in the contest."

I sigh and roll my shoulders as I get up, letting Nicole help me to the bedroom without the crutches. My knee feels much better, and I don't always need them if I can lean on Nicole or Felix a bit when walking short distances in the apartment. Nicole walks into my bedroom at my side and shuts off the lights for me after I settle on the bed.

Even though I have this amazing woman with me, and I know I'm going to make love to her – not just have sex – I can't help but wish the other piece of my heart was here with us.

Dance Battle

Felix

The haze of smoke in the club is almost cloying, and I wave my hand in front of my face. It's Saturday night, and the dance floor is busy. Women in miniskirts and halter tops shimmy their shoulders at me when I walk by, but I ignore them. Five bartenders at both bars can't keep up with the drinks, and the club has opened up a beer trough for people wanting simple bottles of beer. That's new, but it makes me happy people are still enjoying disco on a weekend.

I glance at my watch. Dex should already be here since he told me to meet him twenty minutes ago. Dex is never late, but I am this time.

After having regular lights on when I dance with Nicole and during my classes, it takes my eyes moments to adjust to the disco effect as blue and purple lights dance across every person and surface. The booths are full, and my nose itches as I watch heads lean over the tables with dollar bills ready. "Le Freak" plays at deafening levels, and my shoulders shake to it involuntarily as I make my way to where I think Dex will be. He isn't in his booth, so that means he's probably watching the dancers from the bar.

I look around the club until I spot his crutches leaning against a bar stool. Nobody dares move them for the seat, and I chuckle to myself that I get to be the one he comes home to at night.

Well, I'm the one he comes home to *most* nights. The other person he spends time with is on the dance floor already. I spot her in a blue sequin jumpsuit, a one-piece I've never seen before that suits her. It's tight, fitting like a glove in all the right places. Did Dex buy her a new outfit for coming to the club? I guess it's possible she bought her own since we pay her a salary a little more than her teaching job paid. Maybe she wanted some new, sexier clothes.

"There you are!" Dex says as I walk toward him. He kisses me on the cheek, and I put my hand on his back. The club is one of the places where we can be open and nobody cares. "You ready?"

I pull my spring jacket off and shove it at Dex. "As ready as I'll ever be."

"Just pretend the crowd is the audience at the contest," Dex says.

"I know. I know. Will you order me a gin and tonic while I dance with your girl?"

He nods as I roll my shoulders and unbutton another button on my black dress shirt. As I walk to the dance floor, I feel Dex's approving eyes burning a hole in my tight pants. I stop suddenly before I reach the dance floor and turn my head so fast that I catch him checking me out. When he notices he's been caught, he winks at me.

I take the steps to the dance floor, approach Nicole, and her face falls when she sees me. Damn. That twinges a bit, and I hate the hurt. Resent it even.

"You ready?" I ask, ignoring our feelings. I probably deserve her not skipping for joy when I arrive at the party.

She nods and looks at the DJ, who's noticed me. Dex told me he was paying the man to watch for me and start up our contest song as soon as I got to the dance floor. Nicole presses her forehead to mine in the starting position as we stand in the middle of the dance floor, probably looking like maniacs since we're waiting for our music to start dancing.

"You aren't going to drop me, are you?" she asks. Her breath smells like peppermint, and there's a product in her hair that smells heavenly tonight. My heart pounds at the very smell of her, but I take a deep breath, willing my enjoyment of anything about her to go away.

My eyes meet hers, and we gaze at each other for a few seconds. "No, Nicole. I won't drop you."

"Is it because Dex is watching?"

The music starts and we keep our foreheads together as we start our hip shimmies. "It's because everyone's watching. You ready to be the hottest new thing here?"

Before she can answer, we separate and move into our side-step sequence. People back away from us now as we start what Dex has been calling our "dress rehearsal." He thought it would be a good idea to run through the whole routine on an actual dance floor in front of people who haven't seen it in person or in a mirror a thousand times.

We move into our complicated arm movements and spin, and the crowd cheers and whistles. At this point, they have to know it's a choreographed dance since our matching arm movements and footwork could never be improvised. Nicole does the thigh sit as lights bounce off her sequined outfit, nearly blinding me.

But I can do this dance with her blindfolded. Her body is like clay in my hands, and I know exactly how far to reach for her and on which count. She does the trust fall flawlessly and with so much trust that my heart clenches. Once I right her back to standing, I quickly push her into the spin and pull her up so she can slide down my body. The disco ball lights are jarring, and the screams and whistles are distracting, but I still know exactly where to put my hand so that they connect with hers.

I catch her each and every time I reach out. When I look down, her eyes are open and on mine, and I almost drop her at the emotion in them. She looks at me like I'm her hero. Like I'm Superman and she's Lois Lane.

All I did was catch her.

We separate and do our planned individual movements before coming back together to do our complicated footwork sequence. By the end of our routine, people are nearby, clapping and screaming my name. They don't scream Nicole's because they don't all know it yet, but their eyes roam her body, wanting her and wanting to know who she is.

They'll know her name now, though, and I'm not sure how I feel about it. Am I jealous because they'll associate her with me, and they'll see Dex on her arm? Am I proud that she's my dance partner tonight?

Because I am proud of her. My heart pounds and not from the dancing. My mouth is dry, and I smile despite myself. She's utterly fucking gorgeous tonight, and she's dancing with me.

The song ends, and people I've known for years approach us, patting me on the back. They shake Nicole's hand and ask for her name, and I can't take it. I can't stand there and watch her get all this attention when I'm not sure how to feel about it.

I walk away from her, leaving her on the dance floor. When I turn around to see if she's following me like the lost puppy I expect her to be, I stop suddenly when I see other people asking her to show them some moves. She's still on the dance floor and moving side to side with the transition music the DJ plays between songs as she smiles and chats to everyone like she's the natural star of the show.

Turning back around, I push aside any thoughts of Nicole Tate and stalk to the man I love as he leans against the bar, his eyes on Nicole.

"Well, you should be proud of yourself. You've turned the mousy little thing into a star at the club you love so much," I say as Dex pushes a drink into my hand.

"I didn't do shit. You did that all by yourself," he says. "You made her look like a star up there, and I'll have a hard time holding on to my girl tonight. I should punch you in the dick."

I laugh and look back at Nicole. It's not just men wanting to dance with her as the music segues to the latest ABBA tune. Women flock around her, touching her sequined outfit or fluffing her feathered hair. It's only then that I realize she's had it cut. Did Dex take her, or did she decide on the style by herself? I didn't comment on it, and I should tell her it looks nice.

Scratch that. I should let her think I haven't noticed her change. She looks so...comfortable. Like this was who she's been all along and she just needed a push in the right direction.

"What do you think?" Dex yells over the music and chants as people line the dance floor to watch Nicole.

I lean back against the bar and watch her dance without Dex and without me. People back up and circle her to watch, and I can't help smiling. "She's surprising sometimes, I'll give her that."

"Does that mean you're going to give her a chance?"

I lift my drink and take a long swallow. "I've *been* giving her a chance." On the stage, Nicole shakes her hips and does a punching roll with her arms as she moves across the floor, her face rosy with confidence. "I'll admit that I was a smidge wrong about her, but don't you dare tell her I said that. I'm not ready for that. One good dance under a disco ball does not make a relationship for me."

"I'll never give away the best of you, Felix." He leans his head on my shoulder, and I kiss the top of it. "We have a chance, you know?"

"Chance with what? Being with Nicole or winning the contest?"

"Both," he says. He flicks a lazy hand at the cigarette smoke passing in front of us. "I wanted you to see her tonight. I thought it would be good to nail that routine and then see her through other people's eyes. Not just your clouded ones."

"The competition will be fierce."

He lifts his head and tilts back his own martini. When it's gone, he sucks the olives, as is his habit. "You're a strong leader, and she's come a long way. You can win this. She'll look to you for guidance and comfort for her nerves. You know that, right?"

"I don't know if she will. If you were her partner, yeah, she'd look to you for those things. I don't think she wants any comfort from me, and she's learned I don't give it like you."

He giggles and sets his glass down before kissing me on the cheek. "I'm going to get closer and make sure every man over there knows she's with me. But look at her, man." He nods toward her as she does a point and fancy footwork to go along with it. "Don't underestimate her. We've been surprised at every turn with that one."

Tima Talk

Nicole

Tima blows out a line of smoke, jolting me from my thoughts. "You going to wash those dishes or are you trying to turn your fingers into raisins?" she asks.

I stare down at the dishes in my sink and the barely-there bubbles. I don't know how long I've been standing here and staring into space, my hands idly pushing plates around in the dishpan. My mind has been in a thousand directions lately. Dex. Felix.

Me.

I think about how I've changed more than anything these days. Mostly, I consider how much I like myself now. That's never happened before. There's always been a voice in the back of my head that I was too skinny. Too fat. Too smart. Too dumb. I couldn't be the best in the room because I was taught that the men needed to be the best in the room or at least feel like they were.

If there's one thing meeting Dex and starting work with him has done, it's shown me that I'm smart. My body is fine the way it is. I can also be the best in the room if I'm dancing with Dex...at least, as far as female partners go.

I was taught to put male feelings above my own, and having men put my feelings ahead of theirs is surreal.

Well, at least Dex puts my feelings above his. Felix still drops me on my ass, the difference between the men and how they treat me being night and day.

But something niggles at my brain when I'm with Felix. Something about the way Dex talks about him – reveres him – makes me think that if I can just crack Felix's rough outside demeanor, I think he'll treat me like Dex treats me.

I haven't seen Tima for a week. We keep missing each other because I'm either at work, she's at work, I'm training with Felix, or I'm with Dex. Even with a wrap around his knee, I don't want for anything when I'm with him. He'll hobble to a restaurant with me, even offering me his arm as much as he can with the crutches in the way. He gave me the most orgasmic foot massage the other night as we talked about our hopes for the contest, and he praised me for how far I've come.

I can talk to him about anything.

Almost anything, that is. I can't talk to him about Felix dropping me. I can't put that stress on him. Dex may think the sun shines out of my ass, but he thinks the same of Felix. As much as I could get revenge on Felix by showing Dex the bruise on my butt or telling him the mean words Felix whispers as he spins me, I just can't. I wouldn't let Dex take me from behind the other night, lest he see the marks and question it.

Deep down, there's some spark of hope that I can melt Felix's black heart.

"Penny for your thoughts," Tima says, nudging me aside and turning on the tap. She fills a floral-patterned glass as I watch, mesmerized.

"Sorry, I'm just thinking."

"This Dex guy getting to you?" She waggles her eyebrows.

"Dex is fine. Perfect. It's the other one."

I pull the drain plug and walk to the kitchen table, my arms still dripping wet. Tima throws me a blue dish towel, and I slink into the plastic chair with a squelching sound. She braces her arms on the counter and squints at me. "The other one good, or the other one bad?"

"Bad. He can be an asshole, but I don't think that's really who he is."

She cringes and makes a sucking noise. "Can't have that. It'll end badly for all of you."

I cross my arms and lean back. Maybe I need an objective opinion here. "Alright, what would you do?"

"You don't want advice from me."

"Taking advice from you to go out is why I'm in this pickle. But it brought me to Dex, so I'd like to hear what you suggest."

"I need to know the whole story first."

"Dex and Felix are roommates but...more. They're in love."

Tima tilts her head like she just heard the sweetest bit of gossip since the Nixon tapes. "They're boyfriend and...boyfriend?" she asks, wiggling her index finger like they're in the room and she's pointing at them. "I thought Dex was falling in love with you?"

"He is. He told me."

She lets out a low whistle. "Is that why his boyfriend is being a jerk?"

"I don't know." I shake my head. "They've talked about bringing someone else into their relationship for a long time. They want a family. They want..." My voice trails off, and Tima leans over the counter, holding her breath. "They want more love in their life. Dex would have me living with them if Felix wasn't dragging his feet."

"What's this Felix got against you, anyway?"

I shrug. "I don't think he's liked me since day one. He's one of those guys with an edge and a chip on his shoulder. Dex is a guy who loves anyone he takes a shine to." I rub my nose as it starts to run, and my eyes sting with tears. "The thing is, I adore Felix when he's being nice. That's only when he's around Dex, but he's funny. Sweet. I see how he is with him. I see him through Dex's eyes so much that I question my own judgment. I wish I could make him love me like that."

"Well, you can't."

My head jerks up. "That's it?"

She nods and shrugs, her big earrings swaying with her. "You can't make someone love you."

"Never? Not even if you're super nice to them?" This goes against everything I've ever been told.

"In my experience, being super nice to someone who is dead set on hating you is the worst thing you can do."

"What the hell?" I ask.

She nods. "To get under his skin, you're going to have to act like you're a bad bitch and you don't care about his shit. After that, he may fall all over you to look his way."

"You think I should be mean? Well, not mean, but you think I should just act like I don't care if he likes me. Stop trying?"

"I don't know much, and I can't believe you're asking me for love advice. I mean, you have it with the Dex guy. You should probably be giving me advice." She adjusts her bangle bracelets on her left wrist and sighs. "But love is one of those things that can happen quickly if a person is open to it."

"Dex and I are open to it. Is that why it happened so fast with him?"

"Probably," she says. "But Mr. Dickhead probably isn't as open to it. He's resisting. It almost sounds like he's a perfectionist and doesn't believe in love unless every single star aligns. He probably doesn't see Dex's flaws, but he sure sees yours."

"But I could win him over, right?"

"I guess you could, but are you willing to put in that kind of time without guaranteed results? Are you willing to get too enmeshed with Dex, only to be disappointed when Felix, who's been there longer, puts his foot down and convinces Dex to dump you?"

It's a legitimate question. Am I peeing into the wind by even trying? What's the saying? When someone shows you who they are, you believe them. Hasn't Felix shown me who he is? Why try? Why sit around and worry about Felix?

"What would you do?"

Tima bites her lip and scratches at something on the beat-up counter. "Honestly, Nicole, I'd walk. I'd wash my hands of the whole damn thing. Maybe that's me never being in true love. But if you stay and can't win him over, Felix will cause a rift between you and Dex, and that will create a rift between Dex and Felix. I don't know anything about the world you're dipping your toe into, honey, but I surmise everyone involved has to be all in. If not, it'll be a fucking disaster. Someone will get hurt, and the best thing you can do is to make sure that someone isn't you."

She picks up her water and walks from the room, leaving me with my thoughts. Actually, they're her thoughts because I know she's right. Could I even look in the mirror with the knowledge that I tore Felix and Dex apart? I love Dex so much I couldn't do that to him.

Now I know how that mother in the King Solomon Bible story about the baby felt. I remember it from Sunday school, and I never thought I'd apply it in real life, certainly not about a bisexual couple in Chicago. But I can't help but think about the mother in that story willing to give her baby to another woman to save it. It was an act of true love – giving up what she knew was rightfully hers so it would be protected.

I may be falling in love with Dex, and he may love me, but I can't let him tear his world apart for me. It's not just his relationship with Felix. Felix is Dex's world and part of his business.

As soon as this dance contest is over, I'm telling Dex that I can't be with him. Well, maybe not as soon as it's over. I'll need to find the right time to lessen the hurt. But I can't do this.

To any of us.

The Contest

Felix

"**R**eady?" I ask, my voice trembling. I need to man up and control the fear sinking into my balls.

I take deep breaths, hoping a relaxed demeanor will calm Nicole. Her cheeks are pink, and she nervously taps her toes. The sound makes a clacking sound that sets my teeth on edge, but I won't scold her for it. I can't. We both have the same roiling nerves, and neither one of us wants to let Dex down. I won't dare bark at her and set off her concentration.

"I think so," she mumbles. She cracks her knuckles and acts like my question is intrusive. I can't blame her there. I haven't given her much reason to trust my reactions to conversation.

The room is dim except for the dance area. Spotlights hang in strategic positions around the room, but I can still make out the table of judges against the wall, a bright white tablecloth drawing attention to them since the rest of the room has dark flooring and curtains. It feels odd to disco in something that looks like a ballroom. The judges wear stern expressions like they're jury members in a murder case instead of judging a dance contest. Around us, other dancers in sequined leotards lean against the walls, numbers pinned to our backs and all looking around at the other dancers with nervous eyes.

Dex sits in the third row of the audience. I quickly look at him, and he waves, smiles, and gives us a thumbs-up as Nicole blows out a nervous sigh next to me.

"It'll be fine," I mumble, bumping her shoulder.

Since Dex has been out of commission with teaching any classes that require too much movement on his knee, Nicole's been helpful with rescheduling his classes to meet my schedule and smoothing things over with our clients. I don't know why. You'd think she'd be happy to see the back of me every day after the way I've treated her since we met. She smiles and hands me a cup of coffee every morning. She hasn't given up on me, and she's clearly not giving up on Dex.

If you'd have told me three months ago that this girl has a spark of fight in her, I'd have called you a liar.

I've dropped her on her ass – literally – and she got up every single time. After a while, I know she expected it, but she took the fall, brushed off her butt, squared her shoulders back, and told me to start again. Maybe it was intentional on her end, but dropping her and making her uneasy lost its shine when I couldn't piss her off. She never lashed out, probably for Dex's sake, and she acted like she was above me. This one's not nearly as weak as I pegged her to be.

Was it a fight I was looking for all along? Dex and I were instantly in love, and that's the way he was with Nicole, much to my annoyance. But have I always been looking for the tension I need? Someone to fight with me so that Dex can love me hard right after?

She and Dex have still been seeing each other separately, and Dex and I go to dinner and a movie on nights when he's not with Nicole. I know the stress of keeping us separate is eating at him, though. He puts a bright smile on for me when he comes home from dinner or a movie with her, but it's not like his usual greeting when he comes home. He's overcompensating with me, probably overcompensating with her, and stressed to the max that Nicole and I have to find a way to work and train together.

He smells like her all the time. I'm starting to associate her perfume with his normal smell. I came home one night last week and heard our bed hitting the wall, Dex moaning her name. My hand was on the doorknob, ready to join them like the time we took Nicole's virginity, but I couldn't. I stood there and listened while he made her come, and I listened to the rhythmic sounds of the bed frame hitting the wall while he orgasmed, moaning her name. It sounded so foreign to hear a name other than mine come from his lips during sex.

It also turned me on. I wanted them both so badly, but how could I just saunter into the room after how I treated her?

The funny thing is, I can't help but realize that I'm the problem in this entire bullshit situation, and I'm afraid I'll lose Dex because of it. I know he likes women. I know he wants children. I know he wants the mother of his children in his life. I've always been aware of this, and I *need* him to have these things. Hell, I'd like a child someday. I adore women as much as I love men. So why am I being an asshole to the one woman that's come along who makes him happy and can give everything we want to both of us?

At this point, my pride is too in the way to apologize to either of them, especially Nicole. My hands are on her for hours a day. Lifting. Pulling. Twirling. Her body now feels like it's molded to my fingers when I lift her. After just a few weeks, I'm almost as familiar with her body as I am with Dex's.

Right now, she's scared of a little dance competition. She rubs her thighs together like she desperately needs to go to the bathroom. She holds her shoulders still, but there's a slight tremble to them, and her hands pull at her outfit.

I can't stand to see her nervous and struggling, and that realization tells me how fucked up I am by her, Dex, and their relationship with each other.

The urge hits me like a brick to the face.

Dear God, I want to be somewhere in there.

I'm not sure how I'll fit, but I suddenly *want* to fit into their life. Without Dex at her side, I have an overwhelming urge to protect and reassure her. She's like an annoying sibling who I love to insult, but I'll fucking kill anyone who hurts her.

My mind whirls with psycho-evaluating our group dynamic. Why it happens right this second, when I have a dance competition to win, I don't know, but I let my mind roam to a place I've never explored. Have Nicole and I fallen into a good cop versus bad cop routine to fill the holes in Dex's life without even consulting him first? Why do I want to take over the task of caring for her when Dex isn't around? Because right now, if she'd allow it, I'd pull her to my chest and stroke her hair like I did at the hospital. My fingers twitch at my side with the urge.

On the dance floor, a couple finishes their dance and faces the judges. Still grim-faced and showing zero emotion, the judges mark their sheets with bright yellow pencils. The couple bows one last time and walks from the dance floor.

"We're next," I say, pulling my shoulders back and blowing out my own sigh.

I shake out my legs and make sure my costume looks put together with no sudden tears or wrinkles. My black body suit, popular with dancers and figure skaters the world over, matches Nicole's sequined leotard. My outfit is meant to match hers but showcase the female dancer throughout the routine. Dex wanted nothing outlandish.

I don't know what comes over me, but I slide my hand into hers. She startles at my touch, and I can't blame her. She's not used to me touching her without it being for training, work, or sexual pleasure when we're both pleasing Dex.

She looks down at where our hands are joined and gives a weak smile. The small reassurance from her encourages me to double down, and I squeeze her fingers. "We've got this. Just me and you."

Just us. The sentiment tears through me. Sure, we are helping Dex's business, but this is just Nicole with me out on that dance floor in mere moments. Maybe I'm not as in love with her as I am with Dex, but I want to be happy with her performance, and I want her to be proud of mine.

I look away from her, not ready to deal with these strange new feelings that are so foreign, so completely opposite from what I've shown her.

"Remember what we've practiced, and we'll win," I say as the head judge announces us to polite applause from everyone in the room but Dex, who is clapping like a maniac in his seat.

Reaching the center of the dance floor, Nicole and I face each other, and I push my forehead to hers in starting position. When I wrap my hands around her back, she shivers like she's cold. It's warm in here, so I know she's either nervous or turned on by my hands touching her so intimately. Maybe it's both, and I can't help but feel pleased somewhere in my dark heart.

"It's just me. We've danced with way fewer clothes than this," I joke.

She gives me a half-hearted smile, and I run my fingers up her spine, noticing the instant relaxation. "Dance with me, Nicole. For Dex."

The music starts, and I'm transported to a world where nothing else exists. It's me with Nicole, and I can practically feel Dex's hot gaze as he watches us, a team player even though he isn't doing the dancing. I can't see his face, but I can feel his approval in my bones as Nicole and I finish the sexy shimmy and start our side steps. Our moves are crisp and clean, and a glow of pride and confidence spreads across Nicole's face. Her smile lightens so much that by the time we get to the behind-the-neck arm movements, Nicole's body is fluid, confident, and she lets me lead her.

I smile at her, trying to silently convey she's nailing the routine. It must work because she grinds into me with sass that I, quite frankly, didn't know she possessed. Her shoulders are poised, and a drop of sweat trickles from her temple.

She backs away from me and turns as I shuffle behind her. Our arm movements are in perfect unison, and I'm so busy watching her, amazed at her precision, that I almost mess up.

We simultaneously spin, Nicole falls back into the trust fall without worry, and I catch her in perfect position under her armpits. I pull her into a lift and spin in our circle for two turns before letting her slide down my body. Maybe it's because we're in competition, but she knows I won't drop her this time. Too much is at stake. Frankly, I like it when she trusts me. Maybe I should try to earn it more often.

We complete the side-by-side footwork sequence, and her hand on my shoulder is strong yet relaxed enough so it doesn't look like she gives a fuck what anyone thinks. We smile past the judges, both finding Dex's eyes in the crowd, and his gaze from several yards away burns a hole through me. I'm not even jealous that he's staring at Nicole like she's lunch just as much as he's looking at me.

For the last beats, we face each other one more time, and I pull her to me as she leans back, her tits halfway out of her leotard. It's all I can do not to lean forward and run my tongue down into her cleavage. Maybe find a nipple.

No time for that.

Thunderous applause fills the room as the music ends, and I place a small kiss on Nicole's nose. I press my forehead to hers to finish in starting position, and my smile matches hers.

"You did good, kid. Thanks," I whisper.

She slides her arms around my neck and hugs me tightly. "That was amazing. Thanks for not dropping me, asshole."

"Not in front of people," I reply, hazarding a glance at the judges. Their expressions are still stern, but a couple of them slightly nod as they mark through their sheets. "And I'll never drop you again."

She raises an eyebrow, doubtful. "We'll see."

"My days of dropping you on your ass for kicks are over."

Nicole looks at the crowd, and we both find Dex on his feet and clapping so hard his entire body shakes. Two bouquets, obviously one for each of us, are tucked under his armpit.

I slide my hand into Nicole's again and shudder at how familiar it feels. How right. For the first time, I think about what Dex once said to me.

Nicole Tate feels like home. Just a little.

***

Twenty-three other couples dance after us, and that's in addition to the twenty-six that went before us. I tap my shoes against the linoleum as the judges line up the medals and trophies at the front of the room. The top six teams will get medals, with the top three also getting trophies, a mish-mash of cash prizes, and bragging rights that will skyrocket their studios and businesses for the next year. The trophies don't vary in size, and they look the same from a distance, but I'm sure the place ranking will be engraved on the front of the trophy.

Behind me, Dex stands as close to my back as he can in mixed company. We're in a generally accepting crowd, and we know several dancers in the group who certainly have different partner types, but we're still not going to flaunt our relationship without knowing which judges judge more than dance contests.

Dex's heat whispers against my back, and nerves pulse through my body. Thankfully, Nicole notices and moves next to me until our arms touch. Has she forgiven me? She winds her arm around my waist just as Dex wraps his arms around her from behind. He places a soft kiss on her shoulder. For the first time since I met her, it doesn't bother me that he kisses her. I wonder if people saw me kiss her on the nose and treat her like a lover and are now seeing Dex do it.

We stand in a connected unit, and Dex's finger whispers over my shoulder. "No matter what happens, you did amazing.

We only need the top three to leverage this over the next year. Bragging rights on this can change our lives," Dex says.

"I was so worried I'd mess up and you'd never talk to me again, Dex," Nicole murmurs. I notice she directed it to Dex. She still has issues with me.

Dex squeezes her harder. "Believe me, you earned the fucking I'm going to give both of you later. I mean *both* of you in my bed. None of this one-at-a-time thing. We have some things to hash out."

Before I can comment or even look at Dex to see what he's thinking, the lead judge, a middle-aged man in wire-frame glasses with salt and pepper hair, taps on the microphone. High-pitched feedback fills the silence, and most people cover their ears. My group's hands are otherwise busy, and we don't dare stop touching each other.

My group. The words sucker punch me so hard in the gut as another thought follows it.

My family.

Even her.

"Thank you to all of the attending contestants today," the judge says in a squeaky voice. He may be in charge, but he doesn't like public speaking. "Everyone did well."

"Bullshit," Dex mutters under his breath. "Some people sucked ass."

Nicole elbows him for me, and the man announces the sixth, fifth, and fourth-place winners in succession and hands them their medals and certificates as a *Chicago Tribune* photographer takes a picture of each couple.

With each team called, my hope both plummets and creeps into the clouds. After each announcement, there are fewer spots to place. Honestly, all the teams getting medals did great routines.

"In third place is Debbie Bowsker and Clark Williamson from Oak Park Dance Club Cooperative."

Nicole stiffens next to me. There are only two spots left. One team put the pedal to the floor in their routine with more lifts and technical maneuvers than Nicole and I tried. Maybe if I had fostered trust instead of trying to break her, we could have attempted the same lifts and gasp-inducing maneuvers that only figure skaters are bold enough to attempt.

The third-place winners take their trophy, and the lead judge clears his throat again. "We seem to have a tie for first place, so we've unanimously decided to split the second-place prize money and first-place prize money and give half to both teams. I hope that's an acceptable solution."

My eyes flick to Dex, and Nicole squeezes my waist harder. "Oh, damn," she whispers.

"The first team to win first place is Nola Lane from Midwest Dance Club partnering with Robert Dwyer of Chicago Ballroom."

Around us, people applaud politely as a beautiful woman in her late teens or early twenties with auburn hair walks to the judge's table while she holds hands with a man with dark hair and broad shoulders. They're waved to the side for their pictures, and I look at the floor. Could we have possibly tied with them and their technical moves? We had better choreography with more fancy footwork and arm movements. Artistry counts for a lot, but placing now seems like a pipe dream.

"And last but not least, the other first-place finish is..." The man's words trail off, and I want to punch him in the dick for making us wait. The entire crowd holds its breath. "Nicole Tate and Felix Rathbone representing Holden Dance Studio in Chicago."

I hear applause. I hear my own last name, but it sounds foreign, and not one person in our little group registers the win for at least five seconds. Eyes turn to us, and I feel another competitor's pat on my back, but I still don't move. Then, Nicole and I turn to each other, and our eyes slowly widen at the same exact time. Our mouths open in screams, and we hug each other. I bounce Nicole up and down as Dex wraps us in a bear hug and buries his face into the back of my neck, public eyes be damned.

Eventually, Dex moves back and physically nudges Nicole and me toward the table to get our prize. She trembles more than she did before the dance as I accept the trophy and we both shake the judges' hands.

When it's time for our picture, we stand side-by-side for the newspaper reporter. "Say 'cheese' for the camera," the man in the stereotypical fedora says.

Nicole and I both smile, our arms around each other. "Dex," we both say at the same time.

Lay All Your Love on Us

Nicole

I swipe a dusting cloth down the trophy and position it so it's at an exact ninety-degree angle in its place of prominence near the front door. Anyone who comes through the studio doors will see it. It may be obnoxious, but it's not nearly as bad as the banner out on the street that touts us as an award-winning dance studio.

Award-winning. Dex has been mumbling that word for days while he paces and shakes his head. He's been busy with contractors, two banks, and getting an assistant lined up to start handling a new location's bookings. I certainly can't handle them after all the work I've been doing.

Just like Dex predicted, the studio's business has exploded. The prize money was enough to put a small down payment on a studio in Lincoln Park that Dex will run, but the current studio is bursting at the seams. My ear hurts from using the phone so much. It rings off the hook with new clients and current clients wanting to upgrade their packages. When the studio isn't jam-packed, I do my best to catch up on bookkeeping and cleaning.

I want to leave him in good shape because it will be hard enough to replace me. I don't want to add undo stress on the man I love, but I can't stay here anymore.

He doesn't know yet. We went home from the contest and made love. All of us. I didn't even care when Dex took Felix from behind as Felix took me face-to-face. That was new, too. The first time we all did it, Felix took me from behind. This time, I looked him in the eyes and watched every emotion cross his face.

It scared me.

How can I fall for him when he's been so terrible to me? The more I think about it, my usually clueless roommate was right. I've been looking at Felix through Dex's eyes because I love Dex. Dex loves Felix. I'm not thinking about Felix with my own mind. I'm seeing what Dex sees, even though it's not returned from Felix.

It all makes my head hurt.

I can't be the third wheel. As much as I want to stay and fight for Dex, I won't fight Felix for him. They're in love, and

Felix was here first. Whatever I choose, Dex ends up hurting. It's better to make a clean break now. Maybe the new studio and the success he's having will soothe any heartbreak I serve him.

I haven't seen Felix much since Dex has been sticking to our unspoken *one-date-per-night* rule since the time we celebrated the contest win. Felix has also been so busy with teaching and working with a decorator on the new studio that I haven't seen him except in passing. From our history together, I doubt he'll miss me.

Walking to the coffee pot, I open the container and am about to pick it up to fill with more water, when the door swings open.

Felix walks in and smiles a little when he sees the trophy by the door. "Placing it front and center?" he asks, his voice friendlier than I'm used to.

"He deserves bragging rights," I say.

"We all deserve it."

I give him a weak smile and walk to my desk, and he follows me, probably going to the storage room. He stops suddenly as he eyes the cardboard box on my desk that contains my fern, my most recent knitting project, and the framed picture of my grandmother I'd brought from home.

He scowls at the box and idly picks up my half-knitted scarf. "Going somewhere?"

I pinch my nose and blow out a sigh so hard that my bangs move. "I was going to tell you. I thought I'd get my stuff packed just in case everyone wanted me to leave immediately."

Felix turns to me, and I back up until my shoulders hit the wall. Even when he would drop me on my ass or sneer and snarl with jealousy, I've never seen his face so full of rage. His nostrils flare, and his face reddens. He grits his teeth so hard I worry they'll crack. "Running away? Are you running out on him?"

Hell no. He doesn't get to accuse me of running when he's done everything in his power to make sure I was out of the picture. I swear that I can feel rage ooze from my pores, and I flex my fingers because I didn't realize that my hands were balled into fists.

"No," I growl, and now it's Felix's turn to take a step back. He's never seen me angry. "I'm not running away. You've made it clear that I'm to go away quietly, and I'm hoping Dex is so busy that it won't hurt him as much. You don't get to judge me for it."

"You don't think he'll hurt?"

My heart clenches at the idea of leaving Dex. I love him. With all my heart. I've never loved anyone that way. But if someone needs to back out of this unusual trio, it has to be me. "He has you."

"He wants you, too."

"That's neat. You don't."

Felix's shoulders slump, and he looks at the paper blotter on my desk and toys with my pen cup like he needs something to do with his hands. I let him seethe in silence and wrap his head around my news.

Eventually, he puts his hands on his hips. "Don't go. Don't do this."

Laughter bubbles from my chest, and I cover my mouth with my hand. There's nothing funny about leaving Dex, but Felix telling me not to leave after he's done nothing but encourage me to leave is laughable. "You aren't the boss of me, Felix. Besides, I'm doing this for you."

"Me?" he asked, confused.

"Don't play dumb, Felix. You've hated me since the first time you set eyes on me."

"Don't do this to us!" he yells, jabbing his finger in his chest.

It's my turn to look confused. My face burns with anger. "Us? You don't even like me. You've made it very damn clear, Felix! Congratulations! You're getting exactly what you wanted for the last few months. Me gone."

"You're right! I didn't fucking like you. I thought you were a Mary Sue who never does anything wrong. You've never broken a rule, have you?" He doesn't notice when I shake my head. "You're oil. I'm water. You're cold. I'm hot. I didn't like you because we're so opposite, and you would have never been my first choice for us if I had met you on the street."

"Thank you for finally being honest about how much you hate me!"

"I'm finally starting to love you, God damn it!"

The room spins, and I shake my head, blinking like I've been slapped. "Wh-what the hell? You just said you didn't like me!"

We're both red-faced from yelling. Heat lingers in my cheeks. Part of me worries if the police will be called if the neighbors in the building report it. Dex doesn't need *that* type of marketing.

Felix must also realize it because he drops his voice and takes deep breaths through his nose. He turns in a circle and runs his hands through his hair in frustration.

"I didn't *like* you at first, Nicole. But I can *love* you now. I have been through the wringer of emotions on it, believe me." He pauses, lets out a long exhale, and then smiles at me with actual kindness.

"I still don't understand."

"Apparently, you can still love someone and not have a thing in common with them." He sits on the desk and looks at his feet. "I would never have chosen you. You're the kind of woman I'd see at the club and not glance twice at. I prefer miniskirts and eyeshadow, not peasant tops and lip balm." He runs his hand through his hair and all the way down his face before gripping his shirt with clenched fists. "The new haircut is gorgeous, by the way. It suits you. I didn't want to tell you because I'm a prideful shit you don't deserve."

I want to look away from him, but I can't. His face droops like a sad child's expression before a breakdown.

"I thought Dex was crazy for falling for you. I saw a country mouse that the man I loved also loved. I was confused. Hurt. But one thing Dex has always been good at is knowing what I need. Not necessarily what I want. I didn't want you, Nicole. Well, not at first. But I *need* you. I've learned that over the last three months of working with you, especially when we trained for the contest. We've worked together for hours a day both at the studio and winning that stupid fucking trophy. Somewhere along the line, my heart changed, and I fought and fought to not feel that way because I have too much pride. Does it make you feel good to hear it?"

"You're starting to love me?" I ask in a whisper. "How? When?"

He wipes his face and sighs. "I don't know if I ever would have changed my mind about this crazy arrangement if Dex hadn't hurt his knee. It was that damn dance training when I started to see you differently. I dropped you on your ass in the trust fall. I felt horrible about it, Nicole. Like something woke up inside of me, yawned, and stretched. Then, you had the nerve to ask to practice the trust fall again like you weren't the least bit fucked if I dropped you on your ass again. That was the first time I thought that I may have underestimated you."

"You wouldn't be the first to do that."

He holds up an index finger like he's making an important point. "Dex never has. He's always thought the sun shined out of your ass. I was jealous of you. I was jealous of the possibility of your relationship with Dex. Dex and I have talked about bringing a woman into our relationship for years. I know that's what he wants. I know that I want him to have what he wants. Hell, it's what I want. You rocking that contest a couple weeks ago – that was amazing, and I'll never forget that you did this for Dex and me. Never. I will always love you for it because it was the ultimate act of love for the man we both adore. I love the way you love him, and you don't care one bit that I also love him."

Felix stops and frowns. "Why has it never bothered you, by the way? Most women would care." He furrows his brow like he's confused as he waits for my answer.

"You know him, Felix," I say. "He makes anyone he loves feel like he'd burn down the world for them. I've never had one person, not even my own cold-fish family, ever make me feel like I'm the most important person to them. Even when he was out with you, and I knew you'd go home and have sex, I didn't care because I know he loves me and would have had me with you in bed if you'd allow it. Well...if you wanted me there. I know you'd let Dex do whatever he wants."

He blinks a couple of times and runs his hand down his cheek again. "He loves you, and he loves me. You're infuriating and kind of ridiculous with your bullshit innocence, and I've tried to hate you, but I can't. I can't hate you anymore, Nicole. You're kind, smart, and you bit your lip and gave it hell to win that competition. You never give up, and I respect the fuck out of you for it now. You didn't do it for me. You did it for Dex, and it humbled me to see that.

"I see how he loves you. How you love him," he says, taking a step toward me. "But I hope you can see how he loves me and I love him. We have one hell of a triangle here, but it's love. It's a love triangle, but not the typical kind. I don't want it to be fighting and pushing. I don't want to compete with you. I want to try to love you like he does. I know Dex has always wanted to be in one big fucking circle of love, and I think I finally get it. It's not meant to be a competition, and I've been making it one." His lips move into a smattering of a smile. "If I make another shape reference, you're free to slap me."

He presses his hand to his chest over his heart and clears his throat like he's getting choked up. "Stay. Please."

"For Dex?"

"And me. I want to try."

"Felix Rathbone, have I grown on you?"

He smiles and waves his hand over his shoulder. "Like some unidentified lump on my back," he chuckles. "I think, with time, we can find something we have in common or even work toward it. What I have with Dex is easy. What you have with Dex is easy. But you and I will need to work at it, probably a little bit every day, and I'm OK with that. In fact, it may make all of us stronger."

We both take deep breaths, and tears sting my eyelids. I don't want to leave Dex, and Felix is asking me to stay. Do I give it a go? Is this like a huge trust fall but with my heart as the thing he gets to drop?

Either way, I should try for Dex's sake. If Felix and I can work this out, I have no doubt that I'd have two men who can make me feel special. Safe. I will never be alone. Never ignored.

I also can't go home. Where did I think I was going? Tima's chomping at the bit to move in with Miriam so they can party more, and I won't have a job. I'll have to move back home downstate, and I certainly don't fit there. I left them a quiet, shy girl with no idea who I was or what I wanted. I moved to a big city, only knowing what I'd been told by everyone in a small town my whole life.

Could I really show up there as a woman who's made love to two men, worked at a dance studio, and won first place in a Chicago dance contest? A woman who perseveres when she wants something and talks back when someone disrespects her?

They wouldn't recognize me, and it has nothing to do with my stylish new haircut or the big hoop earrings now in my ears.

I smile a shaky grin at Felix. My chin quivers, and he takes two steps toward me. "We can find something we like to do," I say. "I want to put in the work. For Dex's sake. You can have stuff you do with Dex, and maybe you and I can have a hobby we can bond over."

He's in front of me and tilting my chin up further to him. His chest heaves, but his eyes are kind. "Just out of curiosity, what god-awful hobby do you think we'll find that we both like?"

"Do you like macrame?"

"Shut your filthy fucking mouth," he chuckles, stepping closer.

"Puzzles every Friday night?" I ask, raising my eyebrows.

"I'd rather die."

I open my mouth to suggest ukelele lessons when his mouth is on mine, silencing me. I wrap my arms around his neck and lean into his kiss. It's then that I realize I've never kissed him. He kissed me on the nose during the competition. We've had sex with Dex twice, but I only kissed Dex then, even when I was face-to-face with Felix a couple weeks ago. His lips are so different from Dex's. Harder. Felix is a man who knows what he wants from whomever he's kissing, and he explores and takes what he likes.

Our mouths mesh together, and I lovingly cup his face, stroking his skin with the pads of my fingers. He winces into my mouth a little, and I wonder if I'm a new sensation for him – a feminine touch showing him love. Dex is all hard, whereas I'm soft. Dex may be loving with him, but I'm just...different.

When we break apart, he pushes his nose to mine and closes his eyes. He makes a humming sound, and my hands go to his back, lifting his shirt a bit and feeling the warmth of his skin. It's comforting. I know his body well, but I want to adore it. Snuggle against him. Something tells me he'd allow it this time.

"Want to go tell Dex we aren't going to kill each other?" I ask.

Home at Last

Felix

Her hand is warm in mine. I've held her hand countless times throughout our training, but I didn't appreciate it then. Everything about her is familiar. The shampoo. Her scent. It's the same one left on my sheets after she and Dex screw. I've been going to bed and kissing the man I love on those same sheets every night. Does she know my smell from the same bedding? Does she inhale my lingering soap and cologne when she's with Dex and closes the door to my bedroom?

Our bedroom.

There can be no doubt that Dex will push for her to live with us. Am I ready for it? Maybe. Maybe not. But I know I want to try for the first time in my life. I want to try with someone who isn't Dex, and that's progress, partly because Dex and I have never had to try. Our love was unconditional from the start.

Nicole? This will take work, but I'm finally ready to put it in. That's what most love is, right? Working on it day after day to get it right? It will involve me keeping my mouth shut at times, letting her be who she is, and understanding that Dex loves us both. I know that now. I know it by the way he looks at her. It's the same way he looks at me. But there's no way I can let her walk away from us. I'm enchanted now, too.

I unlock the apartment door. We'll have to give her a key so she can come and go as she pleases, even if she doesn't move in right away. I examine the thought in my mind as I wave her through the front door and into the dim living room. I chuckle to myself that the idea of walking down to the hardware store and making her a key doesn't repulse me like it would have mere weeks ago. It's funny how spending hours of training time with someone and seeing them become the best version of themselves can change your perspective.

"Is he already in bed?" Nicole asks, sliding out of her poncho so she's only wearing a simple short-sleeved shirt.

Months ago, I would have lamented her boring shirt under the brown and white plaid poncho. A simple gold necklace is around her neck. I would have picked something sparkly, more ostentatious, but it suits her. I reach out and trace it with my finger along her collarbone. She shivers into the feeling and glances to watch me as much as she can until my finger trails to the back of her neck. "You deserve something shinier," I say. "Let me get it for you."

She shakes her head. "It's just not me, Felix. Buy something pretty for Dex."

"Let me spoil you. It's what I need sometimes, too. You'll have to let me eventually. I know Dex gives you things, but you deserve it from both of us."

She smiles a wry grin and slides her hand down my chest. The sensation sends chills up my body, and I sharply inhale, already aroused for her in a way I didn't think possible. It's not just sexual. I want her around me. I want to consume her. I want our pent-up jealous energy to explode.

She grabs my hand and leads me to the bedroom. The small table lamp Dex always leaves on for me when I'm out late casts the room into shadow as soon as the door opens.

He stirs on the bed, his eyes fluttering open as Nicole sits next to him and puts her hand on his hip. "Dex, are you awake?"

"Nicole?" he asks, confused. He's confused because he sees her and hears her, but he also sees me behind her with her other arm around my waist, pulling me to the edge of the bed.

"We're here."

"Both of you?" he chuckles and sits up on his elbows, blinking. "I didn't even have to beg. You're in the same room."

"Felix and I talked," Nicole says. "We're going to try. I'm all in, Dex."

His eyes flick to mine, and my legs quiver at the look he gives me. He's only looked at me that way a few times before, and every time was a moment when we realized how incredibly lucky we are to have each other.

"Really?" he asks. He needs to hear it from me.

"Really," I say, nodding.

"Wait. You like her?"

Nicole snorts a laugh. "I wouldn't go that far."

I run my hand through Nicole's hair. "I think I love her. Maybe you're right and she's what we've needed all along. I wasn't ready for her, but I am now."

I hold his eye contact, confirming my words with my expression. "Now that you're giving her a chance, she'll grow on you fast," Dex says.

"So I'm told." I bend down and kiss Nicole on the center of her forehead. "Time will tell on that one."

Dex sits up further and reaches for me. I fall into him and straddle him as he wraps his arms around me, bringing his mouth to mine. After kissing Nicole, the mustache I'm more than familiar with feels rough against me. I cup his cheeks as I hungrily return his kiss. Nicole's hand is on my shoulder, massaging me.

I pull away from Dex and grab Nicole around the waist, pulling her down to us. My mouth finds her, and I kiss her with the same exuberance as what I just shared with Dex. When I finally pull away from her, I let Dex kiss her as I drag my lips and tongue up his salty neck.

A whine comes from his throat, and he pulls both of us further onto the bed. "Show me how much you love her, Felix," Dex whispers, his hand stroking my cheek. "Let me watch you together."

I look at Nicole, and she nods. She playfully pushes Dex onto the bed, and he rolls to his side, propping himself on the bed so he can watch. This obviously isn't so much for arousal as it is making sure Nicole and I can make love by ourselves, with or without him.

And I plan to make love to her with *and* without him for a very long time.

I lay her on the bed and drag my hands to the waistband of her pants. "Take your shirt off for me. Slowly," I direct.

She does as I ask, and I watch the fabric drag over her skin. The stark whiteness of her basic, old-fashioned bra shines almost neon in the dim room, but my eyes don't leave her tits as she reaches behind her back and unhooks it, letting it fall to the side. This show is for me. Dex has made love to her without me, and she's giving this to me and only me for a single moment.

My mouth is on her nipple in seconds, and she arches her back, gasping. Her hands come to my hair, and I make a humming sound against her breast. I push myself between her legs and move to the other nipple, licking and sucking on it until it glistens with my spit.

My hands pull at her jeans, and I make short work of the zipper, dragging it down slowly as I nuzzle her breasts. Dex's hand runs up and down my back, and my mind whirls with sensory overload.

"Mmm. Have I ever told you how I appreciate that you're soft? Dex is so hard, and you're...not," I say, nuzzling her ear.

She opens for me and whines as she circles her hips. "Want something, Nicole?"

"Don't be mean to me. I thought we were past it."

I smile against her cheek as I slide into her inch by inch and stroke her hair. "I'm going to be very nice to you." Her eyes flutter, and her mouth opens as I say it. I cup her face and move my lips next to her ear. "And I'm going to show you exactly what I do to people I love." I pull her legs around me. "You may want to hold on."

I thrust deep inside her, reveling in the tight warmth around my cock and the feel of her hands on my back as she tightens her finger pads against my skin, careful not to scratch me.

"So fucking beautiful watching you together," Dex whispers next to me, but I don't respond. I'm consumed with Nicole. Her smell. The feel of her entire body wrapped around me as I bury myself inside her.

I kiss her neck and her jaw, working my way to her mouth. When our lips touch, she puts her entire body into the kiss, whimpering and bucking her hips as she meets my thrusts. I brace my hand on the headboard and push into her harder and faster as I squeeze my eyes shut and press my forehead to hers like we're in starting position. I've spent so much time like this against her forehead, and it feels familiar and right.

Dex can't help himself and leans forward to capture one of her nipples in his mouth. I run one hand through his hair as he fists himself. To give him clear access, I roll Nicole until she's on top of me.

"Fuck me, Nicole," I beg as I slide into her again.

She's utterly fucking gorgeous as she impales herself all the way onto me and her tits swing with her gentle rocking. Dex runs his tongue up the length of her body and sucks on each breast before kissing his way to her mouth. My hands touch her everywhere I missed when we've fucked before because I didn't want to be too intimate with her then. Her stomach. Her hips. The place where her pelvis meets her thighs. I will not leave this room tonight until I've kissed, mouthed, or touched every inch of her so I can know her as well as I know Dex.

Dex works his mouth back down, and Nicole leans back, grabbing my thighs and throwing her head back at the feel of Dex's mouth now on her clit as she rides me. His tongue hits the root of my cock every so often as he works her, and he smiles up at me.

I grab his hair and buck harder into her pussy. "Get her off for me. I want to feel this pussy come around me and see what all the fuss is."

He buries his face in her slit as far as he can get with my cock still inside of her. Nicole rocks into us both, and I'm unsure which one of us she's enjoying more. She grips my thighs like my legs are stuck in a vice, and she's bent back like a bow so far my cock almost slips out.

"Ride us, Nic," I direct. "Ride my cock and his mouth. You like that? You like being bad?"

"Yes, fuck. Yes, Felix."

Her stomach tenses. I can see it in the position she's in. She whines and rolls her hips as her legs also squeeze my sides, and her nails finally dig into my skin, unable to help herself as her pussy convulses around me with her orgasm.

Dex, for his part, doesn't stop licking and sucking on her. I keep my thrusts steady and don't stop anything I'm doing since she's obviously enjoying it. Her moans fill the room, and my cock is soaked with her pleasure and Dex's spit. I moan a little as I try to control myself. I'm not done with her yet.

Dex finally moves his head, and she flops forward onto me. I still thrust into her, but I hold her tight in my arms as I whisper into her ear how sexy she sounds when she comes for us.

"Think you can take us both?" I ask as Dex drags a single finger down her back. He watches my cock thrust up into her pussy, and I know what he wants.

Nicole lifts her head a bit. "You mean one of you in my butt? I don't think I'm ready for that."

I smile and cup her rosy cheeks. Her hair is askew, and I almost feel sorry for how hard we're about to wear her out. "If I wanted ass, Dex would give it to me. I mean both of us in that pussy now that it's so wet."

She hasn't even consented, and Dex is already in position behind her and between my legs. He waits, though, his chest heaving. He bites his lip with his want, but he won't dare do something so invasive without her permission.

"Will it hurt?" she asks.

"I don't know. I've never had two dicks in my pussy."

She laughs and playfully slaps my cheek.

"But we've done it before to another partner, and she didn't seem to mind. We'll take good care of you after. If you hate it, we can stop and you never have to do it again."

She stares at the pillow by my head for a few seconds as we wait. Dex trembles with anticipation so hard that the bed shakes.

"Do you guys enjoy it?" she whispers.

I run my hand up her arm, letting her get used to a gentle touch before we get a little rough with her. I kiss her jaw. "Dex rubbing his cock against mine inside a woman? How could I not enjoy that?"

"What do I do?" she asks.

"Nothing. We'll move you the way we need, and you can just enjoy it. Do you need something to hold onto?"

She nods, fear in her eyes.

"Hold on to my hair. Grip it hard. I actually like that. But look at Dex," I say, nodding to Dex's face over her left shoulder. "Do you think he'd do anything to hurt you?"

"No," she says, shaking her head.

"If you can't trust me yet, trust Dex."

She inhales deeply and meets my eyes. My heart clenches at how kind those damn green eyes of hers are. "I trust you, Felix."

"Even after all I've done?"

"I forgive you."

I pull her down to me, kissing her again, and her mouth melts into mine. As she's bent over, I pull her ass cheeks apart as Dex thinks better of just getting after it with her. He temporarily leaves and grabs our lube as I kiss Nicole with a hunger I haven't experienced for someone since I first met Dex.

He comes back, and I hear the bottle release air as he squirts the liquid on his cock. His hand rubs the liquid onto his dick, and I jolt when his fingers add some extra lube around Nicole's already wet pussy. He taps my thigh, and I pull out of Nicole just a bit so he can run lube over most of my cock before throwing the bottle aside. I slowly push back inside of her.

Dex pushes against her back and kisses her on the neck. "Just my fingers right now, baby. If you don't like it, say so, and it will stop. Understand?"

She nods and squeezes her eyes shut as Dex slides one finger into her pussy. His knuckle drags against the underside of my dick, and I close my own eyes at the tighter fit and the touch.

"Two now," he says, sliding his index finger in too. He pumps them back and forth, and Nicole takes them both like a champion.

"If you can handle two extra fingers, you can handle a little more. You got this, Nicole. Breathe, OK?" I coo, gripping her hips and pulling her to my chest.

Dex braces his hand next to my head and looks down as he taps his cock against Nicole. Our balls touch, and I nearly come at the warmth as they settle against mine. He pushes the tip of his cock into Nicole, and she gasps.

I grip her hips, holding her in place as Dex slides in a bit more. "Everyone OK?" he asks.

Nicole trembles in my arms but nods. "He's almost all the way there, sweetheart. Just a bit more," I say, my voice husky. Dex's lubed dick sliding against mine as he inches inside her is intense.

He pushes in all the way, and we all sit for a moment, not moving. Dex and I both swivel to get Nicole used to the feel, and she shakes as Dex pulls her up a little. She still holds onto my hair in a death grip, but the sensation just heightens my experience. I can hurt if she's hurting.

I look at Dex over her shoulder and nod. He places a kiss on the nape of her neck before thrusting.

My back arches off the bed, and I whine. My cock is inside Nicole but Dex rubs his dick against mine as he creates friction, threatening to send me over the edge. Nicole doesn't whine or complain. I don't think she'll get off because I'm too overstimulated to focus on her clit for the moment, but she's enjoying it on some level as she rocks her hips against Dex.

He grips her hips and pulls her down more to us. I don't buck or thrust. I throw my head back against the pillow and enjoy the fucking Dex gives us. He's in control and drives both of us as we can do nothing but open our mouths in silent rapture and enjoy the ride.

A tear trickles from my eye at the feel of all of it, and I try to hold myself together, lest I be taken out of the game too quick. Dex's outer thighs tremble against mine. Maybe he feels the same.

"Fuck, Dex," I whine, finally caving first. "Fuck, man, I'm so close. I'm going to fucking come so hard. Fuck her. Fuck us."

He increases his thrusts as Nicole grips my hair even harder. I kiss the inside of her wrist because it's all I can reach. I may bite too. I'm not sure. I can't control my own body, and Nicole's tits flop with Dex's exertions. Moans come from Dex's throat as his own orgasm builds. I know the sounds he makes, and he's in heaven right now.

He goes at us hard as Nicole takes it. "That's our good girl," he says in her ear as his eyes squeeze shut. "That's our girl for doing this for us."

At the last second, Dex's balls flex against mine, and I know that feeling. The sheer depravity and intimacy of our balls twitching against each other as our cocks are buried inside Nicole hit us at the same time. I unload inside of Nicole, gripping her hips and moaning her name as I pull her down and grind her against me. I also moan for Dex. At least, I call out for him in my mind. I'm not sure what comes out of my mouth because my lips barely work as I shake and tremble against Nicole. She massages my chest with one hand through my orgasm. The other hand still pulls at my hair.

Dex comes hard, moaning my name as he leans forward and grips my throat. Our mixed semen drips out of her body and down my balls, tickling as it runs all the way to my ass and over my thighs. His hand on her hip loosens, and she collapses forward onto me with a sigh.

Dex rolls onto his back, settling beside me, both of us coming down from our orgasm. He pulls Nicole onto him, and I help shift her to his chest, missing her skin immediately as soon as she's gone.

Dex's chest still heaves with exertion, and my scalp tingles where she pulled my hair. It's an exquisite hurt, and I run my hand over the painful spots, massaging them, but I'm sure Nicole is sorer than either Dex or I can imagine.

Nicole is on her stomach on top of Dex, and I rise from the bed to get wet washcloths for all of us. When I come back, I hand one to Dex as I clean myself. Then, I take the one meant for Nicole and run the wet rag down her back, circle around to her slit, and swipe back. I hold the cold washcloth over her pussy and coo soothing words, hoping it soothes her. "Is that better?" I whisper.

"Will I get used to you both inside of me at the same time?" she half-laughs. Something in her voice also tells me she's serious.

"Did I hurt you that bad?" Dex asks, tilting her chin so that she's looking at him. He strokes her hair and kisses the top of her head while I kiss a spot between her shoulder blades and lay my head on her lower back.

She purrs at the sensation, shakes her head at Dex's question, and I revel in the warmth of her against my cheek. My hand reaches down, and I clasp Dex's thigh. I know we'll sleep in this position tonight. Nicole is between us, protected from the world by the men that she's somehow managed to find. My head is on her back, and my hand is on Dex's body.

I'm not jealous she's the one curled into his chest. He strokes her hair and then reaches to stroke mine.

My eyes flutter closed, a small smile on my lips as I fall into a dreamless sleep.

September 1980

Dex

"Do you, Dex Holden, take Nicole Tate to be your lawfully wedded wife?"

It's all I can do not to sarcastically snort at the man. I've always wondered – who gets to the altar and changes their mind? It seems ridiculous to me since I have the woman of my dreams in front of me.

To say nothing of the man of my dreams standing right behind me as my best man.

I'd like to say my vows to both of them, but that's not allowed in Illinois...or anywhere, for that matter. It's something I conveyed very seriously to both Nicole and Felix last night as Nicole and I enjoyed our last night with Felix as single people.

And we enjoyed the hell out of it. I knew my day would be all about Nicole and me, so I let Felix have whatever he wanted. He wanted to share Nicole at the same time – the thing he asks for at every birthday or holiday – and we spent time together in the shower this morning, just holding each other in a group hug as the water sprayed down on us.

The marriage certificate is ready to go, but it didn't stop Felix from adding his name in lemon juice, painted with a thin paintbrush one of the third-grade dance students left behind at the studio. He wanted to be on the license, and I'd have his name there with us if I could.

Nicole, for her part, said she'll look at me for half her vows and look at Felix over my left shoulder for the other half. She flew through them with a confident voice, but her eyes watered the entire time.

It's the best we can come up with within the confines of the law.

"I do," I say, just as a fussy squall comes from behind me from the area of Felix's chest.

The witnesses, mostly our dance students and other employees from the studio or at the club, which I just bought from Daniel, giggle and coo at the noise, and the minister smiles.

"It sounds like we have an objection," he jokes, and Nicole leans over me to touch the foot of the baby Felix holds in a sling. She shakes the baby's tiny foot and makes a shushing noise as Felix shifts our gorgeous baby girl, Josi, in his arms.

I smile at the sound of her gurgles and coos, and Felix looks down at the child who is his spitting image.

We were going to get a blood test to see whose daughter she is after she was born. Those aren't certain because the baby could have Nicole's blood type, but we thought we'd try. It doesn't matter in the long run, but we were curious, and she may need to know her medical history in the future. I also had a small bet with Nicole that Josi is mine, but I paid out ten bucks on that one. Once Felix and I saw her in the nursery window, there was no mistake about who fathered her. She's Felix made over, complete with dark curls on her head and the almond shape of her eyes. There's even a small cleft forming on her chin.

Nicole and I may have a child someday, but that will be for a higher power than me to decide. Even if Josi is Felix's biological child, we all equally parent her. Some of my best days are the ones when I take her to work with me and let her crawl around my office. I hold her tiny hands and walk her around the dance floor where I hope she'll take her first steps soon. She loves going everywhere with us, especially into the studio where she watches the disco ball lights with wide eyes, giggling and pointing. Much to my dismay, she doesn't like the softer music or even the disco that's obviously on its way out of style. Josi likes the harder stuff, clapping her hands and giggling whenever Felix plays some of the newer electric-sounding music and even punk.

The minister, an older man in his sixties who is surprisingly cool with our family situation, holds up his hands to the sky. "By the power vested in me by the state of Illinois, I pronounce you husband and wife. You may kiss the bride."

Applause breaks out as organ music plays. Per our prior request, the minister immediately vacates the altar area as I kiss Nicole. He's cool enough to marry us, but we know he's not ready for us all to kiss, and I won't neglect Felix. Neither will Nicole.

I kiss Nicole first. After all, this wedding is for her. For us. It's a special day for her, and I want to make sure she feels loved and like her wedding day is something to be proud of. She smiles and wraps one hand around my neck as Felix moves in for a group hug, careful not to squish Josi against our bodies.

As soon as Nicole and I break our kiss, she kisses Felix full on the mouth. Some in the audience gasp, but it's only one or two people. The rest of the guest list knows exactly what the situation is since we've told them one-by-one over the last two years. There is no more secret keeping from people we come into contact with, especially since the little girl I say is my daughter looks like Felix, complete with curls and chubby cheeks.

In the back of the church, one of Nicole's cousins fans herself and looks away. Nicole invited her entire family. After she explained our relationship and the circumstances, only a few cousins and one of her uncles came. Her parents sent us the stereotypical blender with a card. It said they hope Nicole is happy, but they can't bless our relationship. Felix and I haven't met them, and they only sent a blanket when Josi was born. At the end of the day, it's their loss if they don't want to know their daughter's partners or their own grandchild. We understand the shock, and we're glad some family can participate as they feel comfortable today.

They'll have to get used to it if they stay through the entire reception, though. We've already planned the reception down to the last detail with Nicole and I dancing first and then Felix dancing with her. We'll all cut the cake together, and Felix will sit with us at the head table, me in the middle.

Most of the guest list claps, even as Felix moves his lips to mine as soon as he and Nicole part. Nicole lifts Josi out of the baby sling so I can fully hug Felix.

As Nicole lifts Josi into the air, the little girl giggles and reaches for me. I take her into my arms and wrap her tight as we walk down the aisle, Nicole and Felix flanking me and holding hands.

One happy family. The family Nicole deserves. The family I deserve. The family Felix deserves, even if it took him a little longer to realize it. As much love as we share, it's the family every human soul on Earth deserves because it's real. It's true. It took me a long time to realize that family isn't always blood or what society expects. Love and family are what you make them.

THE END...

Or is it?

***

Thank you for reading *Disco Bar*. Ratings and reviews are so important to indie authors, so please leave a star rating or review on your purchase platform. You can follow me on Instagram and Facebook at @authortoriross to know what I'm working on and if I have a new release!

The Holden story isn't quite over. *Techno Bar* is available to pre-order in eBook format now and will be available in 2025.

On to Josi's story!

2002.

Chicago.

Let's rave.

Also by

Books of Mine to Read if You Liked This One:
Techno Bar: Coming early 2025 (Josi's story)
Rocks
Copper

***

Romantic Comedies:
The Panty Plot
Contact High
Baked and Burned: Coming March 2025
The Cuffing Season Contract: NIEA Award for Romantic
Comedy
All I Wank for Christmas
Winning the Witch

***

The Traveling Calvert Sisters Travel Romance Novellas:
Head Over Heels in Hawaii
Loved in Las Vegas
Christmas on the Cruise Ship
Out of Luck in the Outback
Turkey in Tennessee
Lost in London

***

Erotic Superhero Romance:
Arson
Thirst
Darkness
Amp

***

Erotica:
The Caretaker
The Substitute
The Progressive Dinner

Acknowledgements

This was a hard one, ya'll. Not only was this my first book that was from three points of view, but it was also my first book that I had to stop mid-sentence and research what shampoo was used at the time or something like that. I was two at the time of this book, so this took me vastly longer since I certainly wasn't hanging out in disco clubs in Chicago at the time.

As such, a big thanks to my husband who let me vent about how hard this book was to write. A big thanks to my friends that cheer me on from the sidelines: Lisa, Chrissy, Jaime, Paige, Jess, Nicole N., and the porch-sipping block ladies. Thanks for always asking how it's going. That means the world to a writer.

Thank you to my author friends that help me so much with either marketing ideas or just being a shoulder to cry on: E. L. Koslo, Evie Alexander, Selena Moore, Christian Pan, Indie Sparks, Nat Logan, and Samantha Baca.

Thank you to Tracey Huber. She named Felix by putting the name suggestion into the bucket at Witches in Cottleville all the way back in October of 2022. (Yes, that's how long I've been thinking about this book.)

Thank you to my cool ARC team I now have. Thank you for consistently reading my work. I love all of you.

To my readers that have been with me for the past three years. I love you all so so so much. As long as you keep reading, I'll keep writing.

About Tori Ross

Tori Ross is the Amazon bestselling, Barnes and Noble bestselling, and Apple Top 100 author of several steamy novels, novellas, and shorts. Her book, *The Cuffing Season Contract*, won the National Indie Excellence Award for romantic comedy. She lives in Missouri with her family and two rescue dogs.